SPUTNIK SWEETHEART

Haruki Murakami was born in Kyoto in 1949. His works of fiction include *Dance Dance Dance*, *The Elephant Vanishes*, *Hard-boiled Wonderland and the End of the World*, *A Wild Sheep Chase*, *Norwegian Wood*, *The Wind-Up Bird Chronicle* and *South of the Border, West of the Sun*. His first work of non-fiction, *Underground*, is an exploration of the Tokyo subway gas attack. He has translated into Japanese the work of F. Scott Fitzgerald, Truman Capote, John Irving and Raymond Carver.

Philip Gabriel is Associate Professor of Japanese literature at the University of Arizona. He has translated Haruki Murakami's *South of the Border, West of the Sun* and *Underground* (with Alfred Birnbaum), as well as the work of Senji Kuroi and Masahiko Shimada. He is the co-editor of an anthology of essays, *Oe and Beyond: Fiction in Contemporary Japan*.

ALSO BY HARUKI MURAKAMI

Haruki Murakami

SPUTNIK SWEETHEART

TRANSLATED FROM THE JAPANESE BY
Philip Gabriel

VINTAGE BOOKS
London

Published by Vintage 2002

13 15 17 19 20 18 16 14

Copyright © Haruki Murakami 1999
English translation © Haruki Murakami 2001

Haruki Murakami has asserted his right under the Copyright, Designs and Patents Act 1988 to be identified as the
author of this work

This book is sold subject to the condition that it shall not by
way of trade or otherwise, be lent, resold, hired out, or
otherwise circulated without the publisher's prior consent in
any form of binding or cover other than that in which it is
published and without a similar condition including this
condition being imposed on the subsequent purchaser

First published by Kodansha Ltd in 1999
with the title *Spūtoniku no koibito*

First published in Great Britain in 2001 by
The Harvill Press

Vintage
Random House, 20 Vauxhall Bridge Road,
London SW1V 2SA

www.vintage-books.co.uk

Addresses for companies within The Random House Group Limited
can be found at: www.randomhouse.co.uk/offices.htm

The Random House Group Limited Reg. No. 954009

A CIP catalogue record for this book
is available from the British Library

ISBN 9780099448471

The Random House Group Limited supports The Forest
Stewardship Council (FSC), the leading international forest
certification organisation. All our titles that are printed on
Greenpeace approved FSC certified paper carry the FSC logo.
Our paper procurement policy can be found at
www.rbooks.co.uk/environment.

Mixed Sources
Product group from well-managed
forests and other controlled sources
www.fsc.org Cert no. TT-COC-2139
© 1996 Forest Stewardship Council
FSC

Printed in the UK by CPI Bookmarque, Croydon, CR0 4TD

Sputnik Sweetheart

Sputnik

On 4 October 1957, the Soviet Union launched the world's first man-made satellite, *Sputnik I*, from the Baikanor Space Centre in the Republic of Kazakhstan. *Sputnik* was 58 cm in diameter, weighed 83.6 kilograms, and orbited the Earth in 96 minutes and 12 seconds.

On 3 November of the same year, *Sputnik II* was successfully launched, with the dog Laika on board. Laika became the first living being to leave the Earth's atmosphere, but the satellite was never recovered, and Laika ended up sacrificed for the sake of biological research in space.

from *The Complete Chronicle of World History*

1

In the spring of her twenty-second year, Sumire fell in love
for the first time in her life. An intense love, a veritable
tornado sweeping across the plains – flattening everything in
its path, tossing things up in the air, ripping them to shreds,
crushing them to bits. The tornado's intensity doesn't abate
for a second as it blasts across the ocean, laying waste to
Angkor Wat, incinerating an Indian jungle, tigers and everything, transforming itself into a Persian desert sandstorm,
burying an exotic fortress city under a sea of sand. In short,
a love of truly monumental proportions. The person she fell
in love with happened to be 17 years older than Sumire. And
was married. And, I should add, was a woman. This is where
it all began, and where it all ended. *Almost*.

At the time, Sumire – "Violet" in Japanese – was struggling
to become a writer. No matter how many choices life might
bring her way, it was novelist or nothing. Her resolve was

a regular Rock of Gibraltar. Nothing could come between her and her faith in literature.

After she graduated from a public high school in Kanagawa Prefecture, she entered the liberal arts department of a cosy little private college in Tokyo. She found the college totally out of touch, a lukewarm, dispirited place, and she loathed it – and found her fellow students (which would include me, I'm afraid) hopelessly dull, second-rate specimens. Unsurprisingly, then, just before her junior year, she simply upped and left. Staying there any longer, she concluded, was a waste of time. I think it was the right move, but if I can be allowed a mediocre generalization, don't pointless things have a place, too, in this far-from-perfect world? Remove everything pointless from an imperfect life and it'd lose even its imperfection.

Sumire was a hopeless romantic, a bit set in her ways – innocent of the ways of the world, to put a nice spin on it. Start her talking and she'd go on nonstop, but if she was with someone she didn't get along with – most people in the world, in other words – she barely opened her mouth. She smoked too much, and you could count on her to lose her ticket every time she took the train. She'd get so engrossed in her thoughts at times she'd forget to eat, and she was as thin as one of those war orphans in an old Italian film – like a stick with eyes. I'd love to show you a photo of her, but I don't have any. She hated having her photograph taken – no desire to leave behind for posterity a *Portrait of the Artist as a Young (Wo)Man*. If there were a photograph of Sumire taken at that time, I know it would provide a valuable record of how special certain people can be.

4

I'm getting the order of events mixed up. The woman Sumire fell in love with was named Miu. At least that's what everyone called her. I don't know her real name, a fact that caused problems later on, but again I'm getting ahead of myself. Miu was Korean by nationality, but she didn't speak a word of Korean until she decided to study it when she was in her mid-twenties. She was born and raised in Japan and studied at a music academy in France, so as well as Japanese she was fluent in both French and English. She always dressed well, in a refined way, with expensive yet modest accessories, and she drove a twelve-cylinder, navy-blue Jaguar.

The first time Sumire met Miu, she talked about Jack Kerouac's novels. Sumire was absolutely nuts about Kerouac. She always had her Literary Idol of the Month, and at that point it happened to be the out-of-fashion Kerouac. She carried a dog-eared copy of *On the Road* or *Lonesome Traveler* stuck in her coat pocket, thumbing through them every chance she got. Whenever she came across lines she liked, she'd mark them in pencil and commit them to memory as if they were Holy Writ. Her favourite lines were from the fire lookout section of *Lonesome Traveler*. Kerouac spent three lonely months in a cabin on top of a high mountain, working as a fire lookout.

Sumire especially liked this part:

> *No man should go through life without once experiencing healthy, even bored solitude in the wilderness, finding himself depending solely on himself and thereby learning his true and hidden strength.*

"Don't you just love it?" she said. "Every day you stand on top of a mountain, make a 360° sweep, checking to see if there are any fires. And that's it. You're done for the day. The rest of the time you can read, write, whatever you want. At night scruffy bears hang around your cabin. That's the life! Compared to that, studying literature in college is like biting down on the bitter end of a cucumber."

"Okay," I said, "but someday you'll have to come down off that mountain." As usual, my practical, humdrum opinions didn't faze her.

Sumire wanted to be like a character in a Kerouac novel – wild, cool, dissolute. She'd stand around, hands shoved deep in her coat pockets, her hair an uncombed mess, staring vacantly at the sky through her black plastic-framed Dizzy Gillespie glasses, which she wore despite her 20/20 vision. She was invariably decked out in an oversized herringbone coat from a second-hand shop and a pair of rough work boots. If she'd been able to grow a beard, I'm sure she would have.

Sumire wasn't exactly a beauty. Her cheeks were sunken, her mouth a little too wide. Her nose was on the small side and upturned. She had an expressive face and a great sense of humour, though she hardly ever laughed out loud. She was short, and even in a good mood she talked like she was half a step away from picking a fight. I never knew her to use lipstick or eyebrow pencil, and I have my doubts that she even knew bras came in different sizes. Still, Sumire had something special about her, something that drew people to her. Defining that special something isn't easy, but when you gazed into her eyes, you could always find it, reflected deep down inside.

I might as well just come right out and say it. I was in love with Sumire. I was attracted to her from the first time we talked, and soon there was no turning back. For a long time she was the only thing I could think about. I tried to tell her how I felt, but somehow the feelings and the right words couldn't connect. Maybe it was for the best. If I had been able to tell her my feelings, she would have just laughed at me.

While Sumire and I were friends, I went out with two or three other girls. It's not that I don't remember the exact number. Two, three – it depends on how you count. Add to this girls I slept with once or twice, and the list would be a little longer. Anyhow, while I made love to these other girls, I thought about Sumire. Or at least thoughts of her grazed a corner of my mind. I imagined I was holding her. Kind of a caddish thing to do, but I couldn't help myself.

Let me get back to how Sumire and Miu met.

Miu had heard of Jack Kerouac and had a vague sense that he was a novelist of some kind. What kind of novelist, though, she couldn't recall. "Kerouac . . . hmm . . . Wasn't he a Sputnik?"

Sumire couldn't work out what she meant. Knife and fork poised in mid-air, she gave it some thought. "Sputnik? You mean the first satellite the Soviets sent up, in the fifties? Jack Kerouac was an American novelist. I guess they do overlap in terms of generation . . ."

"Isn't that what they called the writers back then?" Miu asked. She traced a circle on the table with her fingertip, as if rummaging through some special jar full of memories.

"Sputnik . . . ?"

"The name of a literary movement. You know – how they classify writers in various schools of writing. Like Shiga Naoya was in the White Birch School."

Finally it dawned on Sumire. *"Beatnik!"*

Miu lightly dabbed at the corner of her mouth with a napkin. "Beatnik – Sputnik. I never can remember those kinds of terms. It's like the Kenmun Restoration or the Treaty of Rapallo. Ancient history."

A gentle silence descended on them, suggestive of the flow of time.

"The Treaty of Rapallo?" Sumire asked.

Miu smiled. A nostalgic, intimate smile, like a treasured old possession pulled out of the back of a drawer. Her eyes narrowed in an utterly charming way. She reached out and, with her long, slim fingers, gently ruffled Sumire's already tousled hair. It was such a sudden yet natural gesture that Sumire could only return the smile.

Ever since that day, Sumire's private name for Miu was *Sputnik Sweetheart*. She loved the sound of it. It made her think of Laika, the dog. The man-made satellite streaking soundlessly across the blackness of outer space. The dark, lustrous eyes of the dog gazing out of the tiny window. In the infinite loneliness of space, what could Laika possibly be looking at?

This Sputnik conversation took place at a wedding reception for Sumire's cousin at a posh hotel in Akasaka. Sumire wasn't particularly close to her cousin; in fact they didn't get along at all. She'd just as soon be tortured as attend one of these receptions, but she couldn't back out of this one. She and Miu were seated next to each other at one of the tables. Miu didn't go into all the details, but it seemed she'd taught Sumire's cousin the piano – or something along those lines – when she was taking the entrance exams for the university music department. It wasn't a long or very close relationship, clearly, but Miu felt obliged to attend.

In the instant Miu touched her hair, Sumire fell in love, as if she were crossing a field when *bang!* a bolt of lightning zapped her right in the head. Something like an artistic revelation. Which is why, at that point, it didn't matter to Sumire that the person she fell in love with happened to be a woman.

I don't think Sumire ever had what you'd call a lover. In high school she had a few boyfriends, guys she'd go to the cinema with, go swimming with. I couldn't picture any of those relations ever getting very deep. Sumire was too focused on becoming a novelist to really fall for anybody. If she did experience sex – or something close to it – in high school, I'm sure it would have been less out of sexual desire or love than literary curiosity.

"To be perfectly frank, sexual desire has me baffled," she once told me, making a sober face. This was just before she left college, I believe; she'd downed five banana daiquiris and was pretty drunk. "You know – how it all comes about. What's your take on it?"

"Sexual desire's not something you understand," I said, giving my usual middle-of-the-road opinion. "It's just *there*."

She scrutinized me for a while, as if I were some machine running on a previously unheard-of power source. Losing

9

interest, she stared up at the ceiling, and the conversation petered out. No use talking to him about *that*, she must have decided.

Sumire was born in Chigasaki. Her home was near the seashore, and she grew up with the dry sound of sand-filled wind blowing against her windows. Her father ran a dental clinic in Yokohama. He was remarkably handsome, his well-formed nose reminding you of Gregory Peck in *Spellbound*. Sumire didn't inherit that handsome nose, nor, according to her, did her brother. She found it amazing that the genes that had produced that nose had disappeared. If they really were buried for ever at the bottom of the gene pool, the world was a sadder place. That's how wonderful this nose was.

Sumire's father was an almost mythic figure to the women in the Yokohama area who needed dental care. In the examination room he always wore a surgical cap and large mask, so the only thing the patient could see was a pair of eyes and ears. Even so, it was obvious how attractive he was. His beautiful, manly nose swelled up suggestively from under the mask, making his female patients blush. In an instant – regardless of whether their dental plan covered the costs – they fell in love.

Sumire's mother passed away from a congenital heart defect when she was just 31. Sumire hadn't quite turned three. The only memory she had of her mother was a vague one of the scent of her skin. Just a couple of photographs of her remained – a posed photo taken at her wedding, and a snapshot taken immediately after Sumire was born. Sumire used to pull out the photo album and gaze at the pictures.

Sumire's mother was – to put it mildly – a completely forgettable person. A short, humdrum hairstyle, clothes that made you wonder what she could have been thinking, an ill-at-ease smile. If she'd taken one step back, she would have melted right into the wall. Sumire was determined to brand her mother's face on her memory. Then someday she might meet her in her dreams. They'd shake hands, have a nice chat. But things weren't that easy. Try as she might to remember her mother's face, it soon faded. Forget about dreams – if Sumire had passed her mother on the street, in broad daylight, she wouldn't have known her.

Sumire's father hardly ever spoke of his late wife. He wasn't a talkative man to begin with, and in all aspects of life – as though it were a kind of mouth infection he wanted to avoid catching – he never talked about his feelings. Sumire had no memory of ever asking her father about her dead mother. Except for once, when she was still very small, for some reason she asked him, "What was my mother like?" She remembered this conversation very clearly.

Her father looked away and thought for a moment before replying. "She was good at remembering things," he said. "And she had nice handwriting."

A strange way to describe someone. Sumire was waiting expectantly, the snow-white first page of her notebook open, for nourishing words that could have been a source of warmth and comfort – a pillar, an axis, to help prop up her uncertain life here on this third planet from the sun. Her father should have said something that his young daughter could have held on to. But Sumire's handsome father wasn't going to speak those words, the very words she needed most.

*

Sumire's father remarried when she was six, and two years later her younger brother was born. Her new mother wasn't pretty either. On top of which she wasn't so good at remembering things, and her handwriting wasn't any great shakes. She was a kind and fair person, though. That was a lucky thing for little Sumire, her brand-new stepdaughter. No, *lucky* isn't the right word. After all, her father had chosen the woman. He might not have been the ideal father, but when it came to choosing a mate, he knew what he was doing.

Her stepmother's love for her never wavered during her long, difficult years of adolescence, and when Sumire declared she was going to quit college and write novels, her stepmother – though she had her own opinions on the matter – respected Sumire's desire. She'd always been pleased that Sumire loved to read so much, and she encouraged her literary pursuits.

Her stepmother eventually won over her father, and they decided that, until Sumire turned 28, they would provide her with a small stipend. If she wasn't able to make a living by writing then, she'd be on her own. If her stepmother hadn't spoken up in her defence, Sumire might very well have been thrown out – penniless, without the necessary social skills – into the wilderness of a somewhat humourless reality. The Earth, after all, doesn't creak and groan its way around the sun just so human beings can have a good time and a bit of a laugh.

Sumire met her Sputnik Sweetheart a little more than two years after she'd dropped out of college.

She was living in a one-room apartment in Kichijoji where

she made do with the minimum amount of furniture and the maximum number of books. She'd get up at noon, and take a walk around Inogashira Park in the afternoon, with all the enthusiasm of a pilgrim making her way through sacred hills. On sunny days she'd sit on a park bench, chewing on bread, puffing one cigarette after another, reading. On rainy or cold days she'd go into an old-fashioned coffee house where classical music played at full volume, sink down into a worn-out sofa, and read her books, a serious look on her face as she listened to Schubert's symphonies, Bach's cantatas. In the evening she'd have one beer and buy some ready-to-eat food at the supermarket for dinner.

By 11 p.m. she'd settle down at her desk. There'd always be a thermos of hot coffee, a coffee mug (one I gave her on her birthday, with a picture of Snafkin on it), a pack of Marlboro and a glass ashtray. Of course she had a word processor as well. Each key with its very own letter.

A deep silence ensued. Her mind was as clear as the winter night sky, the Big Dipper and North Star in place, twinkling brightly. She had so many things she had to write, so many stories to tell. If she could only find the right outlet, heated thoughts and ideas would gush out like lava, congealing into a steady stream of inventive works the likes of which the world had never seen. People's eyes would pop wide open at the sudden debut of this *Promising Young Writer with a Rare Talent*. A photo of her, smiling coolly, would appear in the arts section of the newspaper, and editors would beat a path to her door.

But it never happened that way. Sumire wrote some works that had a beginning. And some that had an end. But never one that had both a beginning *and* an end.

Not that she suffered from writer's block – far from it. She wrote *endlessly*, everything that came into her head. The problem was that she wrote *too much*. You'd think that all she'd have to do was cut out the extra parts and she'd be fine, but things weren't that easy. She could never decide on the big picture – what was necessary and what wasn't. The following day when she re-read what she'd printed out, every line looked absolutely essential. Or else she'd Tippex out the whole thing. Sometimes, in despair, she'd rip up her entire manuscript and consign it to the bin. If this had been a winter night and the room had had a fireplace, there would have been a certain warmth to it – imagine a scene from *La Bohème* – but Sumire's apartment not only lacked a fireplace, it didn't even have a phone. Not to mention a decent mirror.

On weekends, Sumire would come over to my apartment, drafts of her novels spilling out of her arms – the lucky manuscripts that had escaped the massacre. Still, they made quite a pile. Sumire would show her manuscripts to only one person in the whole world. Me.

In college I'd been two years ahead of her, and our subjects were different, so there wasn't much chance we'd meet. We met by pure chance. It was a Monday in May, the day after a string of holidays, and I was at the bus stop in front of the main gate of the college, standing there reading a Paul Nizan novel I'd found in a second-hand bookshop. A short girl beside me leaned over, took a look at the book, and asked me, Why *Nizan*, of all people? She sounded like she was trying to pick a fight. Like she wanted to kick something and send it flying, but lacking a suitable target had attacked my choice of reading matter.

Sumire and I were very alike. Devouring books came as naturally to us as breathing. Every spare moment we'd settle down in some quiet corner, endlessly turning page after page. Japanese novels, foreign novels, new works, classics, avant-garde to bestseller – as long as there was something intellectually stimulating in a book, we'd read it. We'd hang out in libraries, spend whole days browsing in Kanda, the second-hand bookshop Mecca in Tokyo. I'd never come across anyone else who read so avidly – so deeply, so widely, as Sumire, and I'm sure she felt the same.

I graduated around the time Sumire dropped out of college, and after that she'd hang out at my place two or three times a month. Occasionally I'd go over to her apartment, but you could barely squeeze two people in there, and most of the time she'd end up at mine. We'd talk about the novels we'd read and exchange books. I cooked a lot of dinners. I didn't mind cooking, and Sumire was the kind of person who'd rather go hungry than cook herself. She'd bring me presents from her part-time jobs to thank me. Once she had a job in a warehouse in a drug company and brought me six dozen condoms. They're probably still at the back of a drawer somewhere.

The novels – or fragments of novels, really – Sumire wrote weren't as terrible as she thought. True, at times her style resembled a patchwork quilt sewn by a group of stubborn old ladies, each with her own tastes and complaints, working in grim silence. Add to this her sometimes manic-depressive personality, and things occasionally got out of control. As if this weren't enough, Sumire was dead set on creating a massive nineteenth-century-style Total Novel, a kind of portmanteau packed with every possible phenomenon in order to capture the soul and human destiny.

Having said that, Sumire's writing had a remarkable freshness about it, her attempt to honestly portray what was important to her. On the plus side she didn't try to imitate anyone else's style, and she didn't attempt to distil everything into some precious, clever little pieces. That's what I liked most about her writing. It wouldn't have been right to pare down the direct power in her writing just so it could take on some pleasant, cosy form. There was no need to rush things. She still had plenty of time for detours. As the saying goes, "What's nurtured slowly grows well."

"My head is like some ridiculous barn packed full of stuff I want to write about," she said. "Images, scenes, snatches of words . . . in my mind they're all glowing, all alive. *Write!* they shout at me. A great new story is about to be born – I can feel it. It'll transport me to some brand-new place. Problem is, once I sit at my desk and put them all down on paper, I realize something vital is missing. It doesn't crystallize – no crystals, just pebbles. And I'm not transported anywhere."

With a frown, Sumire picked up her 250th stone and tossed it into the pond.

"Maybe I'm lacking something. Something you absolutely must have to be a novelist."

A deep silence ensued. It seemed she was seeking my run-of-the-mill opinion.

After a while I started to speak. "A long time ago in China

there were cities with high walls around them, with huge, magnificent gates. The gates weren't just doors for letting people in or out, they had greater significance. People believed the city's soul resided in the gates. Or at least that it *should* reside there. It's like in Europe in the Middle Ages when people felt a city's heart lay in its cathedral and central square. Which is why even today in China there are lots of wonderful gates still standing. Do you know how the Chinese built these gates?"

"I have no idea," Sumire answered.

"People would take carts out to old battlefields and gather the bleached bones that were buried there or lay scattered about. China's a pretty ancient country – lots of old battle-grounds – so they never had to search far. At the entrance to the city they'd construct a huge gate and seal the bones up inside. They hoped that by commemorating the dead soldiers in this way they would continue to guard their town. There's more. When the gate was finished they'd bring several dogs over to it, slit their throats, and sprinkle their blood on the gate. Only by mixing fresh blood with the dried-out bones would the ancient souls of the dead magi-cally revive. At least that was the idea."

Sumire waited in silence for me to go on.

"Writing novels is much the same. You gather up bones and make your gate, but no matter how wonderful the gate might be, that alone doesn't make it a living, breathing novel. A story is not something of this world. A real story requires a kind of magical baptism to link the world on this side with the world on the *other* side."

"So what you're saying is that I go out on my own and find my own dog?"

I nodded.

"And shed fresh blood?"

Sumire bit her lip and thought about this. She tossed another hapless stone into the pond. "I really don't want to kill an animal if I can help it."

"It's a metaphor," I said. "You don't have to actually kill anything."

We were sitting as usual side by side at Inogashira Park, on her favourite bench. The pond spread out before us. A windless day. Leaves lay where they had fallen, pasted on the surface of the water. I could smell a bonfire somewhere far away. The air was filled with the scent of the end of autumn, and far-off sounds were painfully clear.

"What you need is time and experience," I said.

"Time and experience," she mused, and gazed up at the sky. "There's not much you can do about time – it just keeps on passing. But experience? Don't tell me that. I'm not proud of it, but I don't have any sexual desire. And what sort of experience can a writer have if she doesn't feel passion? It'd be like a chef without an appetite."

"I don't know where your sexual desire has gone," I said. "Maybe it's just hiding somewhere. Or gone on a trip and forgotten to come home. But falling in love is always a pretty crazy thing. It might appear out of the blue and just grab you. Who knows – maybe even tomorrow."

Sumire turned her gaze from the sky to my face. "Like a tornado?"

"You could say that."

She thought about it. "Have you ever actually seen a tornado?"

"No," I replied. Thankfully, Tokyo wasn't exactly Tornado Alley.

About a half a year later, just as I had predicted, suddenly, preposterously, a tornado-like love seized Sumire. With a woman 17 years older. Her very own Sputnik Sweetheart.

As Sumire and Miu sat there together at the table at the wedding reception, they did what everybody else does in the world in such situations, namely, introduce themselves. Sumire hated her own name and tried to conceal it whenever she could. But when somebody asks you your name, the only polite thing to do is to go ahead and give it.

According to her father, her mother had chosen the name Sumire. She loved the Mozart song of the same name and had decided long before that if she had a daughter that would be her name. On the record shelf in their living room was a record of Mozart's songs, doubtless the one her mother had listened to and, when she was a child, Sumire would carefully lay this heavy LP on the turntable and listen to the song over and over. Elisabeth Schwarzkopf was the soloist, Walter Gieseking on piano. Sumire didn't understand the lyrics, but from the graceful motif she felt sure the song was a paean to the beautiful violets blooming in a field. Sumire loved that image.

In junior high, though, she came across a Japanese translation of the song in her school library and was shocked. The lyrics told of a callous shepherd's daughter trampling down a hapless little violet in a field. The girl didn't even notice she'd flattened the flower. It was based on a Goethe poem, and Sumire found nothing redeeming about it, no lesson to be learned.

"How could my mother give me the name of such an awful song?" said Sumire, scowling.

Miu arranged the corners of the napkin on her lap, smiled neutrally, and looked at Sumire. Miu's eyes were quite dark. Many colours mixed together, but clear and unclouded.

"Do you think the song was beautiful?"

"Yes, the song itself is pretty."

"If the music is lovely, I think that should be enough. After all, not everything in this world can be beautiful, right? Your mother must have loved that song so much the lyrics didn't bother her. And besides, if you keep making that kind of face you're going to get some permanent wrinkles."

Sumire allowed her scowl to relax.

"Maybe you're right. I just felt so let down. I mean, the only tangible sort of thing my mother left me was that name. Other than *myself*, of course."

"Well, I think Sumire is a lovely name. I like it very much," said Miu, and tilted her head slightly as if to view things from a new angle. "By the way, is your father here at the reception?"

Sumire looked around. The reception hall was large, but her father was tall, and she easily spotted him. He was sitting two tables away, his face turned sideways, talking with some short, elderly man in a morning coat. His smile was so trusting and warm it would melt a glacier. Under the light of the chandeliers, his handsome nose rose up softly, like a rococo cameo, and even Sumire, who was used to seeing him, was moved by its beauty. Her father truly belonged at this kind of formal gathering. His mere presence lent the place a flamboyant atmosphere. Like cut flowers in a large vase or a jet-black stretch limousine.

When she spied Sumire's father, Miu was speechless. Sumire could hear the intake of breath. Like the sound of a velvet curtain being drawn aside on a peaceful morning to let in the sunlight to wake someone very special to you. Maybe I should have brought a pair of opera glasses, Sumire mused. But she was used to the dramatic reaction her father's looks brought out in people – especially middle-aged women. What is beauty? What value does it have? Sumire always found it strange. But no one ever answered her. There was just that same immovable effect.

"What's it like to have such a handsome father?" Miu asked. "Just out of curiosity."

Sumire sighed – people could be so predictable. "I can't say I like it. Everybody thinks the same thing: What a handsome man. A real standout. But his daughter, well – she isn't much to look at, is she? That must be what they mean by *atavism*, they think."

Miu turned towards Sumire, pulled her chin in ever so slightly, and gazed at her face, as if she were admiring a painting in an art gallery.

"If that's how you've always felt up till now, you've been mistaken," she said. "You're lovely. Every bit as much as your father." She reached out and, quite unaffectedly, lightly touched Sumire's hand that lay on the table. "You don't realize how very attractive you are."

Sumire's face grew hot. Her heart galloped as loudly as a crazed horse on a wooden bridge.

After this Sumire and Miu were absorbed in their own

private conversation. The reception was a lively one, with the usual assortment of after-dinner speeches (including, most certainly, Sumire's father), and the dinner wasn't half bad. But not a speck of this remained in Sumire's memory. Was the main course meat? Or fish? Did she use a knife and fork and mind her manners? Or eat with her hands and lick the plate? Sumire had no idea.

The two of them talked about music. Sumire was a big fan of classical music and ever since she was small liked to paw through her father's record collection. She and Miu shared similar tastes, it turned out. They both loved piano music and were convinced that Beethoven's Sonata No. 32 was the absolute pinnacle in the history of music. And that Wilhelm Backhaus's unparalleled performance of the sonata for Decca set the interpretive standard. What a delightful, vibrant, and joyous thing it was!

Vladimir Horowitz's mono recordings of Chopin, especially the scherzos, are thrilling, aren't they? Friedrich Gulda's performances of Debussy's preludes are witty and lovely. Gieseking's Grieg is sweet from start to finish. Sviatoslav Richter's Prokofiev is worth listening to over and over – his interpretation exactly captures the mercurial shifts of mood. And Wanda Landowska's Mozart sonatas – so filled with warmth and tenderness it's hard to understand why they haven't received more acclaim.

"What do you do?" asked Miu, once their discussion of music had come to an end.

I dropped out of college, Sumire explained, and I'm doing some part-time jobs while I work on my novels. What kind of novels? Miu asked. It's hard to explain, replied Sumire. Well, said Miu, then what type of novels do you like to read? If I list them all we'll be here for ever, said Sumire.

Recently I've been reading Jack Kerouac. And that's where the Sputnik part of their conversation came in.

Other than some light fiction she read to pass the time, Miu hardly ever touched novels. "I never can get it out of my mind that's it's all made up," she explained, "so I just can't feel any empathy for the characters. I've always been that way." That's why her reading was limited to books that treated reality as reality. Books, for the most part, that helped her in her work.

What kind of work do you do? asked Sumire.

"Mostly it has to do with foreign countries," said Miu. "Thirteen years ago I took over my father's trading company, since I was the oldest child. I'd been studying to be a pianist, but my father passed away from cancer, my mother wasn't strong physically and besides couldn't speak Japanese very well. My brother was still in high school, so we decided, for the time being, that I'd take care of the company. A number of relatives depended on the company for their livelihood, so I couldn't very well just let the company go to pot."

She punctuated all this with a sigh.

"My father's company originally imported dried goods and medicinal herbs from Korea, but now it deals with a wide variety of things. Even computer parts. I'm still officially listed as the head of the company, but my husband and younger brother have taken over so I don't have to go to the office very often. Instead I've got my own private business."

"Doing what?"

"Importing wine, mainly. Occasionally I arrange concerts, too. I travel to Europe quite a bit, since this type of business depends on personal connections. Which is why I'm able, all by myself, to compete with some top firms. But all that networking takes a lot of time and energy. That's only to be expected, I suppose ... " She looked up, as if she had just remembered something. "By the way, do you speak English?"

"Speaking English isn't my strong suit, but I'm okay, I guess. I love to read English, though."

"Do you know how to use a computer?"

"Not really, but I've been using a word processor, and I'm sure I could pick it up."

"How about driving?"

Sumire shook her head. The year she started college she tried reversing her father's Volvo estate into the garage and smashed the door on a pillar. Since then she'd barely driven.

"All right – can you explain, in 200 words or less, the difference between a sign and a symbol?"

Sumire lifted the napkin from her lap, lightly dabbed at her mouth, and put it back. What was the woman driving at? "A sign and a symbol?"

"No special significance. It's just an example."

Again Sumire shook her head. "I have no idea."

Miu smiled. "If you don't mind, I'd like you to tell me what sort of practical skills you have. What you're especially good at. Other than reading a lot of novels and listening to music."

Sumire quietly laid her knife and fork on her plate, stared at the anonymous space hanging over the table, and pondered the question.

"Instead of things I'm good at, it might be faster to list the things I *can't* do. I can't cook or clean the house. My room's a mess, and I'm always losing things. I love music, but I can't sing a note. I'm clumsy and can barely sew a stitch. My sense of direction is the pits, and I can't tell left from right half the time. When I get angry, I tend to break things. Plates and pencils, alarm clocks. Later on I regret it, but at the time I can't help myself. I have no money in the bank. I'm bashful for no reason, and I have hardly any friends to speak of."

Sumire took a quick breath and forged ahead.

"However, I can touch-type really fast. I'm not that athletic, but other than the mumps, I've never been sick a day in my life. I'm always punctual, never late for an appointment. I can eat just about anything. I never watch TV. And other than a bit of silly boasting, I hardly ever make excuses. Once a month or so my shoulders get so stiff I can't sleep, but the rest of the time I sleep like a log. My periods are light. I don't have a single cavity. And my Spanish is okay."

Miu looked up. "You speak Spanish?"

When Sumire was in high school, she spent a month in the home of her uncle, a businessman who'd been stationed in Mexico City. Making the most of the opportunity, she'd studied Spanish intensively. She had taken Spanish in college, too.

Miu grasped the stem of her wineglass between two fingers and lightly turned it, as if turning a screw on a machine. "What would you think about working at my place for a while?"

"Working?" Unsure what expression would best fit this situation, Sumire made do with her usual dour look. "I've never had a real job in my life, and I'm not even sure how to answer a phone the right way. I try to avoid taking the train before 10 a.m. and, as I'm sure you've noticed from talking to me, I don't speak politely."

"None of that matters," said Miu simply. "By the way, are you free tomorrow, around noon?"

Sumire nodded reflexively. She didn't even have to think about it. Free time, after all, was her main asset.

"Well then, why don't we have lunch together? I'll reserve a quiet table at a restaurant nearby," Miu said. She held out the fresh glass of red wine a waiter had poured for her, studied it carefully, inhaled the aroma, then quietly took the first sip. The whole series of movements had the sort of natural elegance of a short cadenza a pianist has refined over the years.

"We'll talk over the details then. Today I'd rather just enjoy myself. You know, I'm not sure where it's from, but this Bordeaux isn't half bad."

Sumire relaxed her dour look and asked Miu straight out: "But you just met me, and you hardly know a thing about me."

"That's true. Maybe I don't," Miu admitted.

"So why do you think I might be of help to you?"

Miu swirled the wine in her glass. "I always judge people by their faces," she said. "Meaning that I like your face, the way you look."

Sumire felt the air around her suddenly grow thin. Her nipples tightened under her dress. Mechanically she reached for a glass of water and gulped it down. A hawk-faced waiter quickly sidled in behind her and filled her empty glass with ice water. In Sumire's confused mind, the clatter of the ice cubes sounded just like the groans of a robber hiding out in a cave.

I must be in love with this woman, she realized with a start. No mistake about it. Ice is cold; roses are red. I'm in love.

And this love is about to carry me off somewhere. The current's too overpowering; I don't have any choice. It may very well be a special place, some place I've never seen before. Danger may be lurking there, something that may end up wounding me deeply, fatally. I might end up losing everything. But there's no turning back. I can only go with the flow. Even if it means I'll be burned up, gone for ever.

Now, after the fact, I know her hunch turned out to be correct. One hundred and twenty per cent on the money.

2

It was about two weeks after the wedding reception when Sumire called me, a Sunday night, just before dawn. Naturally, I was asleep. As dead to the world as an old anvil. The week before I'd been in charge of arranging a meeting and could only snatch a few hours' sleep as I gathered together all the necessary (read *pointless*) documents we needed. Come the weekend, I wanted to sleep to my heart's content. So of course that's when the phone rang.

"Were you asleep?" Sumire asked.

"Um," I groaned and instinctively glanced at the alarm clock beside my bed. The clock had huge fluorescent hands, but I couldn't read the time. The image projected on my retina and the part of my brain that processed it were out of sync, like an old lady struggling, unsuccessfully, to thread a needle. What I could understand was that it was dark all around and close to Fitzgerald's "Dark Night of the Soul".

"It'll be dawn pretty soon."

"Um," I murmured listlessly.

"Right near where I live there's a man who raises roosters. Must have had them for years and years. In half an hour or so they'll be crowing up a storm. This is my favourite time of the day. The pitch-black night sky starting to glow in the east, the roosters crowing for all they're worth like it's their revenge on somebody. Any roosters near you?"

On this end of the telephone line I shook my head slightly.

"I'm calling from the phone box near the park."

"Um," I said. There was a phone box about 200 yards from her apartment. Since Sumire didn't own a phone, she always had to walk over there to call. Just your average phone box.

"I know I shouldn't be calling you this late. I'm really sorry. The time of night when the roosters haven't even started crowing. When this pitiful moon is hanging there in a corner of the eastern sky like a used-up kidney. But think of *me* – I had to trudge out in the pitch dark all the way over here clutching this telephone card I got as a present at my cousin's wedding. With a photo on it of the happy couple holding hands. Can you imagine how depressing that is? My socks don't even match, for pity's sake. One has a picture of Mickey Mouse; the other's plain wool. My room's a complete disaster area; I can't find anything. I don't want to say this too loudly, but you wouldn't believe how awful my panties are. I doubt if even one of those pantie thieves would touch them. If some pervert killed me, I'd never live it down. I'm not asking for sympathy, but it would be nice if you could give me a bit more in the way of a response. Other than those cold interjections of yours – ohs and ums. How about a conjunction? A conjunction would be nice. A *yet* or a *but*."

"However," I said. I was exhausted and felt like I was still in the middle of a dream.

"'However'," she repeated. "Okay, I can live with that. One small step for man. One very small step, *however*."

"So, was there something you wanted?"

"Right, I wanted you to tell me something. That's why I called," Sumire said. She lightly cleared her throat. "What I want to know is what's the difference between a sign and symbol?"

I felt a weird sensation, like something was silently parading through my head. "Could you repeat the question?"

She did. What's the difference between a sign and a symbol?

I sat up in bed, switched the receiver from my left hand to my right. "Let me get this right – you're calling me because you want to find out the difference between a sign and a symbol. On Sunday morning, just before dawn. Um . . . "

"At 4.15, to be precise," she said. "It was bothering me. What could be the difference between a sign and a symbol? Somebody asked me that a couple of weeks ago and I can't get it out of my mind. I was getting undressed for bed, and I suddenly remembered. I can't sleep until I find out. Can you explain it? The difference between a sign and a symbol?"

"Let me think," I said and gazed up at the ceiling. Even when I was fully conscious, explaining things logically to Sumire was never easy. "The emperor is a symbol of Japan. Do you follow that?"

"Sort of," she replied.

"*Sort of* isn't good enough. That's what it says in the Japanese constitution," I said, as calmly as possible. "No

30

room for discussion or doubts. You've got to accept that, or we won't get anywhere."

"Gotcha. I'll accept that."

"Thank you. So – the emperor is a symbol of Japan. But this doesn't mean that the emperor and Japan are equivalent. Do you follow?"

"I don't get it."

"Okay, how about this – the arrow points in one direction. The emperor is a symbol of Japan, but Japan is not the symbol of the emperor. You understand that, right?"

"I *guess*."

"Say, for instance, you write 'The emperor is a sign of Japan.' That makes the two equivalent. So when we say 'Japan', it would also mean 'the emperor', and when we speak of 'the emperor', it would also mean 'Japan'. In other words, the two are interchangeable. Same as saying, '*A* equals *B*, so *B* equals *A*.' That's what a sign is."

"So you're saying you can switch the emperor and Japan? Can you do that?"

"That's not what I mean," I said, shaking my head vigorously at my end of the line. "I'm just trying to explain the best I can. I'm not planning to switch the emperor and Japan. It's just a way of explaining it."

"Hmm," said Sumire. "I think I get it. As an image. It's the difference between a one-way street and a two-way street."

"For our purposes, that's close enough."

"I'm always amazed how good you are at explaining things."

"That's my job," I said. My words seemed somehow flat and stale. "You should try being an elementary-school teacher sometime. You'd never imagine the kinds of questions I get.

31

'Why isn't the world square? Why do squids have ten legs and not eight?' I've learned to come up with an answer to just about everything."

"You must be a great teacher."

"I wonder," I said. I really did wonder.

"By the way, why *do* squids have ten legs and not eight?"

"Can I go back to sleep now? I'm whacked. Just holding this phone I feel like I'm holding up a crumbling stone wall."

"You know," said Sumire, and let a delicate pause intervene – like an old gatekeeper closing the railway-crossing gate with a clatter just after the train bound for St Petersburg has passed by – "it's really silly to say this, but I'm in love."

"Um," I said, changing the receiver back to my left hand. I could hear her breathing down the phone. I had no idea how I should respond. And, as so often happens when I don't know what to say, I let slip some totally inappropriate comment. "Not with me, I assume?"

"Not with you," Sumire answered. I heard the sound of a cheap lighter lighting a cigarette. "Are you free today? I'd like to talk more."

"You mean, about your falling in love with someone other than me?"

"Right," she said. "About my falling passionately in love with somebody other than you."

I clamped the phone between my head and shoulder and stretched. "I'm free in the evening."

"I'll be over at five," Sumire said. And then added, as if an afterthought: "Thank you."

"For what?"

"For being nice enough to answer my question in the middle of the night."

I gave a vague response, hung up, and turned out the light. It was still pitch black out. Just before I fell asleep, I thought about her final *thank you* and whether I'd ever heard those words from her before. Maybe I had, once, but I couldn't recall.

Sumire arrived at my apartment a little before five. I didn't recognize her. She'd taken on a complete change of style. Her hair was short in a stylish cut, her fringe still showing traces of the scissors' snips. She wore a light cardigan over a short-sleeve, navy-blue dress and a pair of black enamel, medium-high heels. She even had stockings on. *Stockings?* Women's clothes weren't exactly my field of expertise, but it was clear that everything she wore was pretty expensive. Dressed like this, she looked polished and lovely. It was quite becoming, to tell the truth. Though I preferred the old, outrageous Sumire. To each his own.

"Not bad," I said, giving her a complete once-over. "But I wonder what good old Jack Kerouac would say."

Sumire smiled, an ever-so-slightly more sophisticated smile than usual. "Why don't we go for a walk?"

We walked side by side down University Boulevard towards the station and stopped by our favourite coffee shop. Sumire ordered her usual slice of cake along with her coffee. It was a clear Sunday evening near the end of April. The flower shops were full of crocuses and tulips. A gentle breeze blew, softly rustling the hems of young girls' skirts and wafting over the leisurely fragrance of young trees.

I folded my hands behind my head and watched Sumire as she slowly yet eagerly devoured her cake. From the small speakers on the ceiling of the coffee shop Astrud Gilberto sang an old bossa nova song. "Take me to Aruanda," she sang. I closed my eyes, and the clatter of the cups and saucers sounded like the roar of a far-off sea. Aruanda – what's it like there? I wondered.

"Still sleepy?"

"Not any more," I answered, opening my eyes.

"You feel okay?"

"I'm fine. As fine as the Moldau River in spring."

Sumire gazed for a while at the empty plate that had held her slice of cake. She looked at me.

"Don't you think it's strange that I'm wearing these clothes?"

"I guess."

"I didn't buy them. I don't have that kind of money. There's a story behind them."

"Mind if I try to guess the story?"

"Go ahead," she said.

"There you were in your usual crummy Jack Kerouac outfit, cigarette dangling from your lips, washing your hands in some public toilet, when this five-foot one-inch woman rushed in, all out of breath, dressed to the nines, and said, 'Please, you've got to help me! No time to explain, but I'm being chased by some awful people. Can I exchange clothes with you? If we swap clothes I can give them the slip. Thank God we're the same size.' Just like some Hong Kong action flick."

Sumire laughed. "And the other woman happened to wear a size-six-and-a-half shoe and a size-seven dress. Just by coincidence."

"And right then and there you changed clothes, down to your Mickey Mouse knickers."

"It's my socks that are Mickey Mouse, not my knickers."

"Whatever," I said.

"Hmm," Sumire mused. "Actually, you're not too far off."

"How far?"

She leaned across the table. "It's a long story. Would you like to hear it?"

"Since you've come all the way over here to tell me, I have a distinct feeling it doesn't matter if I do or not. Anyway, go right ahead. Add a prelude, if you'd like. And a 'Dance of the Blessed Spirits'. I don't mind."

She began to talk. About her cousin's wedding reception, and about the lunch she had had with Miu in Aoyama. And it *was* a long tale.

3

The day after the wedding, a Monday, was rainy. The rain began to fall just after midnight and continued without a stop till dawn. A soft, gentle rain that darkly dampened the spring earth and quietly stirred up the nameless creatures living in it.

The thought of meeting Miu again thrilled Sumire, and she found it hard to concentrate. She felt as though she were standing alone on the summit of a hill, the wind swirling around her. She settled down at her desk as usual, lit a cigarette, and switched on her word processor, but stare as she might at the screen, not a single sentence came to her. For Sumire that was next to impossible. She gave up, turned off the word processor, lay down in her tiny little room, and, an unlit cigarette dangling from her lips, gave herself up to some aimless musings.

If just the thought of seeing Miu has me this worked up,

she thought, imagine how painful it would be if we'd said goodbye at the party and never saw each other again. Am I just yearning to be like her – a beautiful, refined older woman? No, she decided, that can't be it. When I'm beside her, I always want to touch her. That's a bit different from a yearning.

Sumire sighed, gazed up at the ceiling for a while, and lit her cigarette. It's pretty strange if you think about it, she thought. Here I am in love for the first time in my life, aged 22. And the other person just *happens* to be a woman.

The restaurant Miu had made a reservation at was a ten-minute walk from the Omote Sando subway station. The kind of restaurant that's hard for first-timers to find; certainly not a place where you just casually drop in for a meal. Even the restaurant's name was hard to remember unless you heard it a couple of times. At the entrance Sumire told them Miu's name and was escorted to a small, private dining room on the first floor. Miu was already there, sipping an iced Perrier water, deep in conversation with the waiter about the menu.

Over a navy-blue polo shirt Miu had on a cotton sweater of the same colour, and she wore a thin, plain silver hairpin. Her trousers were white slim-fit jeans. On a corner of the table rested a pair of bright blue sunglasses, and on the chair next to her was a squash racquet and a Missoni sports bag. It looked like she was on her way home after a couple of afternoon games of squash. Her cheeks were still flushed a faint pink. Sumire imagined her in the shower at the gym, scrubbing her body with an exotic smelling bar of soap.

As Sumire entered the room, dressed in her usual

herringbone jacket and khaki trousers, her hair all messy like some orphan, Miu looked up from the menu and gave her a dazzling smile. "You told me the other day that you can eat anything, right? I hope you don't mind if I go ahead and order for us."

Of course not, Sumire replied.

Miu ordered the same thing for both of them. The main course was a light grilled fish with a touch of green sauce with mushrooms. The slices of fish were cooked to perfection, browned in an almost artistic way that you knew was *just right*. Pumpkin gnocchi and a delicate endive salad rounded off the meal. For dessert they had the crème brûlée, which only Sumire ate. Miu didn't touch it. Finally, they had espresso. Sumire observed that Miu took great care over what she ate. Her neck was as slender as the stalk of some plant, her body without an ounce of detectable fat. She didn't seem to have to diet. Even so, it would appear she was super-strict about food. Like some Spartan holed up in a mountain fortress.

As they ate they chatted about nothing in particular. Miu wanted to know more about Sumire's background, and she obliged, answering the questions as honestly as she could. She told Miu about her father, her mother, the schools she had attended (all of which she loathed), the prizes she had won in a composition contest – a bicycle and a set of encyclopedias – how she came to quit college, the way she spent her days now. Not a particularly thrilling life. Even so, Miu listened, enthralled, as if listening to the enchanting customs of a far-off land.

Sumire wanted to know so much more about Miu, but

Miu hesitated to talk about herself. "That's not important," she deferred with a bright smile. "I'd rather hear more about *you*."

By the time they finished eating, Sumire still hadn't learned much. About the only thing she found out was this: that Miu's father had donated a lot of money to the small town in the north part of Korea where he had been born, and had built several public buildings for the townspeople – to which they'd responded by erecting a bronze statue of him in the town square.

"It's a small town deep in the mountains," Miu explained. "The winter's awful, and just looking at the place makes you shiver. The mountains are craggy and reddish, full of bent trees. Once, when I was little, my father took me there. When they unveiled the statue. All these relatives came up, crying and hugging me. I couldn't understand a word they said. I remember being frightened. For me it was a town in a foreign country I'd never set eyes on before."

"What kind of statue was it?" asked Sumire. She'd never known anyone who'd had a statue erected.

"Just a normal statue. The kind you'd find anywhere. But it's weird to have your own father become a statue. Imagine if they erected a statue of your father in the square in front of Chigasaki Station. You'd feel pretty weird about it, right? My father was actually fairly short, but the statue made him look like some towering figure. I was only five at the time, but I was struck by the way things you see aren't always true to life."

If they made a statue of my father, Sumire mused, it'd be the statue that would draw the short straw. Since in real life her father was a little *too* good-looking.

"I'd like to pick up where we left off yesterday," Miu began, when they were on their second cup of espresso. "So, do you think you might want to work for me?"

Sumire was dying for a cigarette, but there weren't any ashtrays. She made do with a sip of chilled Perrier.

She answered honestly. "Well, what kind of work would it be, exactly? Like I said yesterday, except for some simple physical-labour-type jobs, I've never once had what you'd call a proper job. Plus I don't have a thing to wear that would be appropriate. The clothes I had on at the reception I borrowed."

Miu nodded, her expression unchanged. She must have anticipated this sort of response.

"I think I understand pretty much what sort of person you are," she said, "and the work I have in mind shouldn't give you any trouble. I'm sure you can handle whatever comes up. What really matters is whether or not you'd like to work with me. Just approach it that way, as a simple yes or no."

Sumire chose her words carefully. "I'm really happy to hear you say that, but right now what's most important for me is writing novels. I mean, that's why I left college."

Miu looked across the table straight at Sumire. Sumire sensed that quiet look on her skin and felt her face grow warm.

"Do you mind if I say exactly what's on my mind?" Miu asked.

"Of course not. Go right ahead."

"It might make you feel bad."

To show she could handle it, Sumire pursed her lips and looked into Miu's eyes.

"At this stage in your life I don't think you're going to write anything worthwhile, no matter how much time you put into your novels," said Miu, calmly but firmly. "You've got the talent. I'm sure someday you'll be an extraordinary writer. I'm not just saying this, I truly believe it. You have that natural ability within you. But now's not the time. The strength you need to open that door isn't quite there. Haven't you ever felt that way?"

"Time and experience," said Sumire, summing it up.

Miu smiled. "At any rate, come and work for me. That's the best choice for you. And when you feel the time is right, don't hesitate to chuck it all in and write novels to your heart's content. You just need more time than the average person in order to reach that stage. So even if you get to 28 without any breaks coming your way, and your parents cut off your funds and you're left without a penny, well – so what? Maybe you'll go a little hungry, but that might be a good experience for a writer."

Sumire opened her mouth, about to reply, but nothing emerged. She merely nodded.

Miu stretched out her right hand towards the middle of the table. "Let me see your hand," she said.

Sumire reached out her right hand and Miu grasped it, as if enveloping it. Her palm was warm and smooth. "It's not something you should worry about so much. Don't look so glum. We'll get along fine."

Sumire gulped, but somehow managed to relax. With Miu gazing right at her like that, she felt as though she were steadily shrinking. Like a block of ice left out in the sun, she might very well disappear.

"Starting next week I'd like you to come to my office

three times a week. Monday, Wednesday, and Friday. You can start at 10 a.m., and you can leave at four. That way you'll miss the rush hour. I can't pay you much, but the work is easy, and you can read when there's nothing to do. One condition is that you take private lessons in Italian twice a week. You already know Spanish, so it shouldn't be too hard. And I'd like you to practise English conversation and driving whenever you have the time. Do you think you can do that?"

"I think so," Sumire replied. Her voice sounded like it was somebody else's coming from another room. No matter what I'm asked to do, no matter what I'm ordered to do, all I can do is say yes, she realized. Miu gazed steadily at Sumire, still holding her hand. Sumire could make out clearly her own figure reflected deep inside Miu's dark eyes. It looked to her like her own soul being sucked into the other side of a mirror. Sumire loved that vision, and at the same time it frightened her.

Miu smiled, charming lines appearing at the corners of her eyes. "Let's go to my place. There's something I want to show you."

4

The summer holiday of my first year in college I took a random trip by myself around the Hokuriku region, came across a woman eight years older than me who was also travelling alone, and we spent one night together. It struck me, at the time, as something straight out of the opening of Soseki's novel *Sanshiro*.

The woman worked in the foreign exchange section of a bank in Tokyo. Whenever she had some time off, she'd grab a few books and set out on her own. "Much less tiring to travel alone," she explained. She had a certain charm, which made it hard to work out why she'd have any interest in someone like me – a quiet, skinny 18-year-old college kid. Still, sitting across from me in the train, she seemed to enjoy our harmless banter. She laughed out loud a lot. And – unusually – I chattered away. We happened to get off at the same station at Kanazawa.

"Do you have a place to stay?" she asked.

"No," I replied. I'd never made a hotel reservation in my life.

"I have a hotel room," she told me. "You can stay if you like. Don't worry about it," she went on, "it costs the same whether there's one or two people staying."

I was nervous the first time we made love, which made things awkward. I apologized to her.

"Aren't we polite!" she said. "No need to apologize for every little thing."

After her shower she threw on a dressing gown, grabbed two cold beers from the fridge, and handed one to me.

"Are you a good driver?" she asked.

"I just got my licence, so I wouldn't say so. Just average."

She smiled. "Same with me. I think I'm pretty good, but my friends don't agree. Which makes me average, too, I suppose. You must know a few people who think they're great drivers, right?"

"Yeah, I guess I do."

"And there must be some who aren't very good."

I nodded. She took a quiet sip of beer and gave it some thought.

"To a certain extent those kinds of things are inborn. Talent, you could call it. Some people are nimble; others are all thumbs . . . Some people are quite attentive, and others aren't. Right?"

Again I nodded.

"Okay, consider this. Say you're going to go on a long journey with someone by car. And the two of you will take turns driving. Which type of person would you choose? One who's a good driver, but inattentive, or an attentive person who's not such a good driver?"

"Probably the second one," I said.

"Me, too," she replied. "What we have here is very similar. Good or bad, nimble or clumsy – those aren't important. What's important is being attentive. Staying calm, being alert to things around you."

"Alert?" I asked.

She just smiled and didn't say anything.

A while later we made love a second time, and this time it was a smooth, congenial ride. *Being alert* – I think I was starting to get it. For the first time I saw how a woman reacts in the throes of passion.

The next morning after we ate breakfast together, we went our separate ways. She continued her trip, and I continued mine. As she left she told me she was getting married in two months to a man from work. "He's a very nice guy," she said cheerily. "We've been going out for five years, and we're finally going to make it official. Which means I probably won't be making any trips by myself any more. This is it."

I was still young, certain that this kind of thrilling event happened all the time. Later in life I realized how wrong I was.

I told Sumire this story a long time ago. I can't remember why it came up. It might have been when we were talking about sexual desire.

"So what's the point of your story?" she asked me.

"The part about being alert," I replied. "Not prejudging things, listening to what's going on, keeping your ears, heart, and mind open."

"Hmm," Sumire replied. She seemed to be mulling over my paltry sexual affair, perhaps wondering whether she could incorporate it into one of her novels.

"Anyway, you certainly have a lot of experiences, don't you?"

"I wouldn't say a *lot*," I gently protested. "Things just *happen*."

She chewed lightly at her nail, lost in thought. "But how are you supposed to become attentive? The critical moment arrives, and you say okay, I'm going to be alert and listen carefully, but you can't just be good at those things by snapping your fingers, right? Can you be more specific? Give me a for instance?"

"Well, first you have to relax. By . . . say, counting."

"What else?"

"Think about a cucumber in a fridge on a summer after-noon. Just an example."

"Wait a second," she said with a significant pause. "Do you mean to tell me that when you're having sex with a girl you imagine cucumbers in a fridge on a summer afternoon?"

"Not all the time," I said.

"But sometimes."

"Maybe."

Sumire frowned and shook her head a couple of times. "You're a lot weirder than you look."

"Everybody's got something weird about them," I said.

"In the restaurant, as Miu held my hand and gazed deep into my eyes, I thought about cucumbers," Sumire said to me. "Gotta stay calm, gotta listen carefully, I told myself."

"*Cucumbers?*"

"Don't you remember what you told me – about cucum-bers in a fridge on a summer afternoon?"

"Oh, yeah, I guess I did," I recalled. "So did it help?"

"A little," she said.

"Glad to hear it," I replied.

Sumire steered the conversation back on track. "Miu's apartment is just a short walk from the restaurant. Not a very big place, but really lovely. A sunny veranda, houseplants, an Italian leather sofa, Bose speakers, a set of prints, a Jaguar in the garage. She lives there alone. The place she and her husband have is somewhere in Setagaya. She goes back there at the weekends. Most of the time she stays in her apartment in Aoyama. What do you think she showed me there?"

"Mark Bolan's favourite snakeskin sandals in a glass case," I ventured. "One of the invaluable legacies without which the history of rock and roll cannot be told. Not a single scale missing, his autograph on the arch. The fans go nuts."

Sumire frowned and sighed. "If they invent a car that runs on stupid jokes, you could go far."

"Put it down to an impoverished intellect," I said humbly.

"Okay, all joking aside, I want you to give it some serious thought. What do you think she showed me there? If you get it right, I'll pay the bill."

I cleared my throat. "She showed you the gorgeous clothes you have on. And told you to wear them to work."

"You win," she said. "She has this rich friend with clothes to spare who's just about the same size as me. Isn't life strange? There are people who have so many leftover clothes they can't stuff them all in their wardrobe. And then there are people like me, whose socks never match. Anyway, I don't mind. She went over to her friend's house and came

47

back with an armful of these *leftovers*. They're just a bit out of fashion if you look carefully, but most people wouldn't notice."

I wouldn't know no matter how closely I looked, I told her.

Sumire smiled contentedly. "The clothes fit me like a glove. The dresses, blouses, skirts – everything. I'll have to take in the waist a bit, but put a belt on and you'd never know the difference. My shoe size, fortunately, is almost the same as Miu's, so she let me have some pairs she doesn't need. High heels, low heels, summer sandals. All with Italian names on them. Handbags, too. And a little make-up."

"A regular Jane Eyre," I said.

All of which explains how Sumire started working three days a week at Miu's office. Wearing a suit jacket and dress, high heels, and a touch of make-up, taking the morning commuter train from Kichijoji to Harajuku. Somehow I just couldn't picture it.

Apart from her office at her company in Akasaka, Miu had her own small office at Jingumae. There she had her desk as well as her assistant's (Sumire's, in other words), a filing cabinet, a fax, a phone, and a PowerBook. That's all. It was just one room in an apartment building and came with an afterthought-type of tiny kitchen and bathroom. There was a CD player, mini-speakers, and a dozen classical CDs. The room was on the second floor, and out of the east-facing window you could see a small park. The ground floor of the building was taken up by a showroom selling Northern European furniture. The whole building was set back from the main thoroughfare, which kept traffic noise at a minimum.

As soon as she arrived at the office, Sumire would water the plants and get the coffee-maker going. She'd check phone messages and e-mails on the PowerBook. She'd print out any messages and put them on Miu's desk. Most of them were from foreign agents, in either English or French. She'd open any ordinary post that came and throw away whatever was clearly junk mail. A few calls would come in every day, some from abroad. Sumire would take down the person's name, number, and message and relay these to Miu on her cellphone.

Miu usually showed up around one or two in the afternoon. She'd stay an hour or so, give Sumire various instructions, drink coffee, make a few calls. Letters that required a reply she'd dictate to Sumire, who'd type them up on the word processor and either post or fax them. These were usually quite brief business letters. Sumire also made reservations for Miu at the hairdresser, restaurants, and the squash court. Business out of the way, Miu and Sumire would chat for a while, and then Miu would leave.

So Sumire was often alone in the office, talking to no one for hours, but she never felt bored or lonely. She'd review her twice-a-week Italian lessons, memorizing the irregular verbs, checking her pronunciation with a tape recorder. She took some computer classes and got to where she could handle most simple glitches. She opened up the information in the hard drive and learned the general outlines of the projects Miu had going.

Miu's main work was exactly as she had described it at the wedding reception. She contracted with small wine producers, mostly in France, and wholesaled their wine to restaurants and speciality shops in Tokyo. On occasion she arranged concert trips by musicians to Japan. Agents from large firms handled the complex business angles, with Miu taking care of the overall plan and some of the ground-work. Miu's speciality was searching out unknown, promising young performers and bringing them to Japan.

Sumire had no way of knowing how much profit Miu made from her private business. Accounting records were kept on separate disks and couldn't be accessed without a password. At any rate, Sumire was ecstatic, her heart aflutter, just to be able to meet Miu and talk to her. That's the desk where Miu sits, she thought. That's the ballpoint pen she uses; the mug she drinks coffee from. No matter how trivial the task, Sumire did her best.

Every so often Miu would invite Sumire out for dinner. Since her business involved wine, Miu found it necessary to regularly make the rounds of the better-known restaurants to stay in touch with the latest news. Miu always ordered a light fish dish or, on occasion, chicken, though she'd leave half, and would pass on dessert. She'd pore over every detail of the wine list before deciding on a bottle, but would never drink more than a glass. "Go ahead and have as much as you like," she told Sumire, but there was no way Sumire could finish that much. So they always ended up with half a very expensive bottle of wine left, but Miu didn't mind.

"It's such a waste to order a whole bottle of wine for just the two of us," Sumire said to Miu one time. "We can barely finish half."

"Don't worry." Miu laughed. "The more we leave behind, the more people in the restaurant will be able to try it. The sommelier, the headwaiter, all the way down to the waiter who fills the water glasses. That way a lot of people will start to acquire a taste for good wine. Which is why leaving expensive wine is never a waste."

Miu examined the colour of the 1986 Médoc and then, as if savouring some nicely turned out prose, carefully tasted it.

"It is the same with anything – you have to learn through your own experience, paying your own way. You can't learn it from a book."

Taking a cue from Miu, Sumire picked up her glass and very attentively took a sip, held it in her mouth, and then swallowed it. For a moment an agreeable aftertaste remained, but after a few seconds this disappeared, like morning dew on a summer leaf. All of which prepared the palate for the next bite of food. Every time she ate and talked with Miu, Sumire learned something new. Sumire was amazed by the overwhelming number of things she had yet to learn.

"You know I've never thought I wanted to be somebody else," Sumire blurted out once, perhaps urged on by the more-than-usual amount of wine she'd drunk. "But sometimes I think how nice it would be to be like you."

Miu held her breath for a moment. Then she picked up her wineglass and took a sip. For a second, the light dyed her eyes the crimson of the wine. Her face was drained of its usual subtle expression.

"I'm sure you don't know this," she said calmly, returning her glass to the table. "The person here now isn't the real me. Fourteen years ago I became half the person I used to be. I wish I could have met you when I was whole – that would have been wonderful. But it's pointless to think about that now."

Sumire was so taken aback she was speechless. And missed the chance to ask the obvious questions. What had happened to Miu 14 years ago? Why had she become half her real self? And what did she mean by *half*, anyway? This enigmatic announcement, in the end, only made Sumire more and more smitten with Miu. What an awesome person, she thought.

Through fragments of conversation Sumire was able to piece together a few facts about Miu. Her husband was Japanese, five years older and fluent in Korean, the result of two years as an exchange student in the economics department of Seoul University. He was a warm person, good at what he did, in point of fact the guiding force behind Miu's company. Even though it was originally a family-run business, no one ever said a bad word about him.

Ever since she was a little girl, Miu had had a talent for playing the piano. Still in her teens she had won the top prize at several competitions for young people. She went on to a conservatoire, studied under a famous pianist and, through her teacher's recommendation, was able to study at a music academy in France. Her repertoire ran mainly from the late Romantics, Schumann and Mendelssohn, to Poulenc, Ravel, Bartók, and Prokofiev. Her playing combined a keen, sensuous tone with a vibrant, impeccable technique. In her student days she held a number of concerts, all well received. A bright future as a concert pianist looked assured. During her time abroad, though, her father fell ill, and Miu shut the lid of her piano and returned to Japan. Never to touch a keyboard again.

"How could you give up the piano so easily?" Sumire

asked hesitantly. "If you don't want to talk about it, that's okay. I just find it – I don't know – a little unusual. I mean, you had to sacrifice a lot of things to become a pianist, didn't you?"

"I didn't sacrifice a *lot of things* for the piano," Miu said softly. "I sacrificed *everything*. The piano demanded every ounce of flesh, every drop of blood, and I couldn't refuse. Not even once."

"Weren't you sorry to give up? You'd almost made it."

Miu gazed into Sumire's eyes searchingly. A deep, steady gaze. Deep within Miu's eyes, as if in a quiet pool in a swift stream, wordless currents vied with one another. Only gradually did these clashing currents settle.

"I'm sorry," Sumire apologized. "I'll mind my own business."

"It's all right. I just can't explain it well."

They didn't talk about it again.

Miu didn't allow smoking in her office and hated people to smoke in front of her, so after she began the job Sumire decided it was a good chance to quit. Being a two-packs-of-Marlboro-a-day smoker, though, things didn't go so smoothly. After a month, like some animal that's had its furry tail sliced off, she lost her emotional grip on things – not that this was so firm to begin with. And as you might guess, she started calling me all the time in the middle of the night.

"All I can think about is having a smoke. I can barely sleep, and when I do sleep I have nightmares. I'm constipated. I can't read, can't write a line."

"Everybody goes through that when they try to stop. In the beginning at least," I said.

"You find it easy to give opinions as long as it's about other people, don't you?" she snapped. "You've never had a cigarette in your life."

"Hey, if you can't give your opinion about other people, the world would turn into a pretty scary place, wouldn't it? If you don't think so, just look up what Joseph Stalin did."

On the other end of the line Sumire was silent for a long time. A heavy silence like dead souls on the Eastern Front.

"Hello?" I asked.

She finally spoke up. "Truthfully, though, I don't think it's because I stopped smoking that I can't write. It might be one reason, but that's not all. What I mean is stopping smoking is just an excuse. You know: 'I'm stopping smoking; that's why I can't write. Nothing I can do about it.'"

"Which explains why you're so upset?"

"I guess," she said, suddenly meek. "It's not just that I can't write. What really upsets me is I don't have confidence any more in the act of writing itself. I read the stuff I wrote not long ago, and it's boring. What could I have been thinking? It's like looking across the room at some filthy socks tossed on the floor. I feel awful, realizing all the time and energy I wasted."

"When that happens you should call somebody up at three in the morning and wake him up – *symbolically* of course – from his peaceful semiotic sleep."

"Tell me," said Sumire, "have you ever felt confused about what you're doing, like it's not right?"

"I spend more time being confused than not," I answered.

"Are you serious?"

"Yep."

Sumire tapped her nails against her front teeth, one of her many habits when she was thinking. "I've hardly ever felt confused like this before. Not that I'm always confident, sure of my talent. I'm not that nervy. I know I'm a haphazard, selfish type of person. But I've never been confused. I might have made some mistakes along the way, but I always felt I was on the right path."

"You've been lucky," I replied. "Like a long spell of rain right after you plant rice."

"Maybe you're right."

"But at this point, things aren't working out."

"Right. They aren't. Sometimes I get so frightened, like everything I've done up till now is wrong. I have these realistic dreams and snap wide awake in the middle of the night. And for a while I can't work out what's real and what isn't . . . That kind of feeling. Do you have any idea what I'm saying?"

"I think so," I replied.

"The thought hits me a lot these days that maybe my novel-writing days are over. The world's crawling with stupid, innocent girls, and I'm just one of them, self-consciously chasing after dreams that'll never come true. I should shut the piano lid and come down off the stage. Before it's too late."

"Shut the piano lid?"

"A metaphor."

I switched the receiver from my left hand to my right. "I *am* sure of one thing. Maybe you aren't, but I am. Someday you'll be a fantastic writer. I've read what you've written, and I know."

"You really think so?"

"From the bottom of my heart," I said. "I'm not going to lie to you about things like that. There are some pretty remarkable scenes in the things you've written so far. Say you were writing about the seashore in May. You can hear the sound of the wind in your ears and smell the salt air. You can feel the soft warmth of the sun on your arms. If you wrote about a small room filled with tobacco smoke, you can bet the reader would start to feel like he can't breathe. And his eyes would sting. Prose like that is beyond most writers. Your writing has the living, breathing force of something natural flowing through it. Right now that hasn't all come together, but that doesn't mean it's time to – shut the lid on the piano."

Sumire was silent for a good 10, 15 seconds. "You're not just saying that to make me feel better, to cheer me up, are you?"

"No, I'm not. It's an undeniable fact, plain and simple."

"Like the Moldau River?"

"You got it. Just like the Moldau River."

"Thank you," she said.

"You're welcome," I replied.

"Sometimes you're just the sweetest thing. Like Christmas, summer holidays and a brand-new puppy all rolled into one."

Like I always do when somebody praises me, I mumbled some vague reply.

"But one thing bothers me," she added. "Someday you'll get married to some nice girl and forget all about me. And I won't be able to call you in the middle of the night whenever I want to. Right?"

"You can always call during the day."

"Daytime's no good. You don't understand anything, do you?"

"Neither do *you*," I protested. "Most people work when the sun's up and turn out the light at night and go to sleep." But I might as well have been reciting some pastoral poems to myself in the middle of a pumpkin patch.

"There was this article in the paper the other day," she continued, completely oblivious. "It said that lesbians are born that way; there's a tiny bone in the inner ear that's completely different from other women's and that makes all the difference. Some small bone with a complicated name. So being a lesbian isn't acquired; it's genetic. An American doctor discovered this. I have no idea why he was doing that kind of research, but ever since I read about it I can't get the idea out of my mind of this little good-for-nothing bone inside my ear, wondering what shape my own little bone is."

I had no idea what to say. A silence descended on us as sudden as the instant fresh oil is poured into a large frying pan.

"So you're sure what you feel for Miu is sexual desire?" I asked.

"A hundred per cent sure," Sumire said. "When I'm with her that bone in my ear starts ringing. Like delicate seashell wind chimes. And I want her to hold me, let everything take its course. If that isn't sexual desire, what's flowing in my veins must be tomato juice."

"Hmm," I said. What could I possibly say to that?

"It explains *everything*. Why I don't want to have sex with any men. Why I don't feel anything. Why I've always thought I'm different from other people."

"Mind if I give you my pennyworth here?" I asked.

"Okay."

"Any explanation or logic that explains everything so easily has a hidden trap in it. I'm speaking from experience. Somebody once said if it's something a single book can explain, it's not worth having explained. What I mean is don't leap to any conclusions."

"I'll remember that," Sumire said. And the call ended, somewhat abruptly.

I pictured her hanging up the receiver, walking out of the telephone box. By my clock it was 3.30. I went to the kitchen, drank a glass of water, snuggled back in bed, and closed my eyes. But sleep wouldn't come. I drew the curtain aside, and there was the moon, floating in the sky like some pale, clever orphan. I knew I wouldn't get back to sleep. I brewed a fresh pot of coffee, pulled a chair over next to the window, and sat there, munching on some cheese and crackers. I sat, reading, waiting for the dawn.

5

It's time to say a few words about myself.

Of course this story is about Sumire, not me. Still, I'm the one whose eyes the story is told through – the tale of who Sumire is and what she did – and I should explain a little about the narrator. Me, in other words.

I find it hard to talk about myself. I'm always tripped up by the eternal *who am I?* paradox. Sure, no one knows as much pure data about me as *me*. But when I talk about myself, all sorts of other factors – values, standards, my own limitations as an observer – make me, the *narrator*, select and eliminate things about me, the *narratee*. I've always been disturbed by the thought that I'm not painting a very objective picture of myself.

This kind of thing doesn't seem to bother most people. Given the chance, they're surprisingly frank when they talk about themselves. "I'm honest and open to a ridiculous degree," they'll say, or "I'm thin-skinned and not the type who gets along easily in the world," or "I'm very good at sensing others' true feelings." But any number of times I've seen people who say they're easily hurt or hurt other people for no apparent reason. Self-styled honest and open people, without realizing what they're doing, blithely use some self-serving excuse to get what they want. And those who are "good at sensing others' true feelings" are taken in by the most transparent flattery. It's enough to make me ask the question: how well do we really know ourselves?

The more I think about it, the more I'd like to take a rain check on the topic of *me*. What I'd like to know more about is the objective reality of things *outside* myself. How important the world outside is to me, how I maintain a sense of equilibrium by coming to terms with it. *That's* how I'd grasp a clearer sense of who I am.

These are the kinds of ideas I had running through my head when I was a teenager. Like a master builder stretches taut his string and lays one brick after another, I constructed this viewpoint – or philosophy of life, to put a bigger spin on it. Logic and speculation played a part in formulating this viewpoint, but for the most part it was based on my own experiences. And speaking of experience, a number of painful episodes taught me that getting this viewpoint of mine across to other people wasn't the easiest thing in the world.

The upshot of all this is that when I was young I began to draw an invisible boundary between myself and other people. No matter who I was dealing with, I maintained a set distance, carefully monitoring the person's attitude so that they wouldn't get any closer. I didn't easily swallow what other people told me. My only passions were books and music. As you might guess, I led a lonely life.

My family isn't anything special. So blandly normal, in fact, I don't know where to begin. My father graduated from a local university with a degree in science and worked in the research lab of a large food manufacturer. He loved golf, and every Sunday he was out on the course. My mother was crazy about tanka poetry and often attended poetry recitals. Whenever her name was in the poetry section of the newspaper, she'd be happy as a lark for days. She liked cleaning, but hated cooking. My sister, five years older than me, detested both cleaning and cooking. Those are things other people did, she decided, not her. Which meant that ever since I was old enough to be in the kitchen, I made all my own meals. I bought some cookbooks and learned how to make almost everything. I was the only child I knew who lived like that.

I was born in Suginami, but we moved to Tsudanuma in Chiba Prefecture when I was small, and I grew up there. The neighbourhood was full of white-collar families just like ours. My sister was always top of her class; she couldn't stand not being the best and didn't step one inch outside her sphere of interest. She never – not even once – took our dog for a walk. She graduated from Tokyo University law school and passed the bar exam the following year, no mean feat. Her husband is a go-getter management consultant. They live in a four-room condo they purchased in an elegant building near Yoyogi Park. Inside, though, the place is a pigsty.

I was the opposite of my sister, not caring much about studying or my grades. I didn't want any grief from my parents, so I went through the motions of going to school, doing the minimum amount of study and homework to get by. The rest of the time I played football and sprawled on my bed when I got home, reading one novel after another. None of your typical after-hours cram school, no tutor. Even so, my grades weren't half bad. At this rate, I reckoned I could get into a decent college without killing myself studying for the entrance exams. And that's exactly what happened.

I started college and lived by myself in a small apartment. Even when I was living at home in Tsudanuma I hardly ever had a heart-to-heart conversation with my family. We lived together under one roof, but my parents and sister were like strangers to me, and I had no idea what they wanted from life. And the same held true for them – they didn't have any idea what kind of person I was or what I aspired to. Not that I knew what I wanted in life – I didn't. I loved reading novels to distraction, but didn't write well enough to be a novelist; being an editor or a critic was out, too, since my tastes ran to extremes. Novels should be for pure personal enjoyment, I decided, not part of your work or study. That's why I didn't study literature, but history. I didn't have any special interest in history, but once I began studying it I found it an engrossing subject. I didn't plan to go to grad school and devote my life to history or anything, though my adviser did suggest that. I enjoyed reading and thinking, but I was hardly the academic type. As Pushkin put it:

> He had no itch to dig for glories
> Deep in the dirt that time has laid.

All of which didn't mean I was about to find a job in a normal company, claw my way through the cut-throat competition, and advance step by step up the slippery slopes of the capitalist pyramid.

So, by a process of elimination, I ended up a teacher. The school is only a few stations away by train. My uncle happened to be on the board of education in that town and asked me whether I might want to be a teacher. I hadn't taken all the required teacher-training classes, so I was hired as an assistant teacher, but after a short period of screening I qualified as a proper teacher. I hadn't planned on being a teacher, but after I actually became one I discovered a deeper respect and affection for the profession than I ever imagined I'd have. More accurately, really, I should say that I happened to discover *myself*.

I'd stand at the front of the classroom, teaching my primary-school charges basic facts about language, life, the world, and I'd find that at the same time I was teaching myself these basic facts all over again – filtered through the eyes and minds of these children. Done the right way, this was a refreshing experience. Profound, even. I got along well with my pupils, their mothers, and my fellow teachers.

Still the basic questions tugged at me: Who am I? What am I searching for? Where am I going?

The closest I came to answering these questions was when I talked to Sumire. More than talking about myself, though, I listened attentively to her, to what she said. She threw all sorts of questions my way, and if I couldn't come up with an answer, or if my response didn't make sense, you'd better believe she let me know. Unlike other people she *honestly, sincerely* wanted to hear what I had to say. I did my best to answer her, and our conversations helped me open up more about myself to her – and, at the same time, to myself.

We used to spend hours talking. We never got tired of talking, never ran out of topics – novels, the world, scenery, language. Our conversations were more open and intimate than any lovers'.

I imagined how wonderful it would be if indeed we *could* be lovers. I longed for the warmth of her skin on mine. I pictured us married, living together. But I had to face the fact that Sumire had no such romantic feelings for me, let alone sexual interest. Occasionally she'd stay over at my apartment after we'd talked into the small hours, but there was never even the slightest hint of romance. Come 2 or 3 a.m. and she'd yawn, crawl into bed, sink her face into my pillow, and fall fast asleep. I'd spread out some bedding on the floor and lie down, but I couldn't sleep, my mind full of fantasies, confused thoughts, self-loathing. Sometimes the inevitable physical reactions would cause me grief, and I'd lie awake in misery until dawn.

It was hard to accept that she had almost no feelings, maybe none at all, for me as a man. This hurt so bad at times it felt like someone was gouging out my guts with a knife. Still, the time I spent with her was more precious than anything. She helped me forget the undertone of loneliness in my life. She expanded the outer edges of my world, helped me draw a deep, soothing breath. Only Sumire could do that for me.

In order to ease the pain and, I hoped, eliminate any sexual tension between me and Sumire, I started sleeping with other women. I'm not saying I was a big hit with women; I wasn't. I wasn't what you'd call a ladies' man, and laid no claim to any special charms. For whatever reason, though, some women were attracted to me, and I discovered that if I let things take their course it wasn't so hard to get them to sleep with me. These little flings never aroused much passion in me; they were, at most a kind of comfort.

I didn't hide my affairs from Sumire. She didn't know every little detail, just the basic outlines. It didn't seem to bother her. If there was anything in my affairs that was troubling, it was the fact that the women were all older and either were married or had fiancés or steady boyfriends. My most recent partner was the mother of one of my pupils. We slept together about twice a month.

"That may be the death of you," Sumire warned me once. And I agreed. But there wasn't much I could do about it.

One Saturday at the beginning of July my class had an outing. I took all 35 of my pupils mountain climbing in Okutama. The day began with an air of happy excitement, only to descend into total chaos. When we reached the summit, two children discovered they'd forgotten to pack their lunches in their backpacks. There weren't any shops around, so I had to split my own *nori-maki* lunch the school had provided. Which left me with nothing to eat. Someone gave me some chocolate, but that was all I had the whole day. On top of which one girl said she couldn't walk any more, and I had to carry her piggyback all the way down the mountain. Two boys started to scuffle, half in fun, and one of them fell and banged his head on a rock. He got a slight concussion and a heavy nosebleed. Nothing critical, but his

65

shirt was covered in blood as if he'd been in a massacre. Like I said, total chaos.

When I got home I was as exhausted as an old railway sleeper. I took a bath, downed a cold drink, snuggled into bed too tired to think, turned off the light, and settled into a peaceful sleep. And then the phone rang: a call from Sumire. I looked at my bedside clock. I'd only slept for about an hour. But I didn't grumble. I was too tired to complain. Some days are like that.

"Can I see you tomorrow afternoon?" she asked.

My woman friend was coming to my place at 6 p.m. She was supposed to park her red Toyota Celica a little way down the road. "I'm free till four," I said.

Sumire had on a sleeveless white blouse, a navy-blue mini skirt, and a tiny pair of sunglasses. Her only accessory was a small plastic hairclip. An altogether simple outfit. She wore almost no make-up, exposed to the world in her natural state. Somehow, though, I didn't recognize her at first. It had only been three weeks since we last met, but the girl sitting across from me at the table looked like someone who belonged to an entirely different world from the Sumire I knew. To put it mildly, she was thoroughly beautiful. Something inside her was blossoming.

I ordered a small glass of draught beer, and she asked for grape juice.

"I hardly recognize you these days," I said.

"It's that season," she said disinterestedly, sipping at her drink through a straw.

"What season?" I asked.

"A delayed adolescence, I guess. When I get up in the

66

morning and see my face in the mirror, it looks like someone else's. If I'm not careful, I might end up left behind."

"So wouldn't it be better to just let it go, then?" I said.

"But if I lost myself, where could I go?"

"If it's for a couple of days, you can stay at my place. You'd always be welcome – the you who lost *you*."

Sumire laughed.

"All joking aside," she said, "where in the world could I be heading?"

"I don't know. Look on the bright side – you've stopped smoking, you're wearing nice clean clothes – even your socks match now – and you can speak Italian. You've learned how to judge wines, use a computer, and at least for now go to sleep at night and wake up in the morning. You must be heading somewhere."

"But I still can't write a line."

"Everything has its ups and downs."

Sumire screwed up her lips. "Would you call what I'm going through a defection?"

"Defection?" For a moment I couldn't see what she meant.

"Defection. Betraying your beliefs and convictions."

"You mean getting a job, dressing nicely, and giving up writing novels?"

"Right."

I shook my head. "You've always written because you wanted to. If you don't want to any more, why should you? Do you think your not writing is going to cause a village to burn to the ground? A ship to sink? The tides to get messed up? Or set the revolution back five years? Hardly. I don't think anybody's going to label that *defection*."

"So what should I call it?"

I shook my head again. "The word *defection*'s too old-fashioned. Nobody uses it any more. Go to some leftover commune, maybe, and people might still use the word. I don't know the details, but if you don't want to write any longer, that's up to you."

"Commune? Do you mean the places Lenin made?"

"Those are called kolkhoz. There aren't any left, though."

"It's not like I want to give up writing," Sumire said. She thought for a moment. "It's just that when I try to write, I can't. I sit down at my desk and nothing comes – no ideas, no words, no scenes. *Zero*. Not too long ago I had a million things to write about. What in the world's happening to me?"

"You're asking me?"

Sumire nodded.

I took a sip of my cold beer and gathered my thoughts. "I think right now it's like you're positioning yourself in a new fictional framework. You're preoccupied with that, so there's no need to put your feelings into writing. Besides, you're too busy."

"Do *you* do that? Put yourself inside a fictional framework?"

"I think most people live in a fiction. I'm no exception. Think of it in terms of a car's transmission. It's like a transmission that stands between you and the harsh realities of life. You take the raw power from outside and use gears to adjust it so everything's all nicely in sync. That's how you keep your fragile body intact. Does this make any sense?"

Sumire gave a small nod. "And I'm still not completely adjusted to that new framework. That's what you're saying?"

"The biggest problem right now is that you don't know

68

what sort of fiction you're dealing with. You don't know the plot; the style's still not set. The only thing you do know is the main character's name. Nevertheless, this new fiction is reinventing who you are. Give it time, it'll take you under its wing, and you may very well catch a glimpse of a new world. But you're not there yet, which leaves you in a precarious position."

"You mean I've taken out the old transmission, but haven't quite finished bolting down the new one? And the engine still's running. Right?"

"You could put it that way."

Sumire made her usual sullen face and tapped her straw on the hapless ice in her drink. Finally she looked up.

"I understand what you mean by *precarious*. Sometimes I feel so – I don't know – lonely. The kind of helpless feeling when everything you're used to has been ripped away. Like there's no more gravity, and I'm left to drift in outer space with no idea where I'm going."

"Like a little lost Sputnik?"

"I guess so."

"But you do have Miu," I said.

"At least for now."

For a while silence reigned.

"Do you think Miu is seeking that, too?" I asked.

Sumire nodded. "I believe she is. Probably as much as I am."

"Physical aspects included?"

"It's hard to say. I can't get a handle on it yet. What her feelings are, I mean. Which makes me feel lost and confused."

"A classical conundrum," I said.

In place of an answer, Sumire screwed up her lips again.

"But as far as you're concerned," I said, "you're ready to go."

Sumire nodded once, unequivocally. She couldn't have been more serious. I sank back deep into my chair and clasped my hands behind my head.

"After all this, don't start to hate me, okay?" Sumire said. Her voice was like a line from an old black-and-white Jean-Luc Godard movie, filtering in just beyond the frame of my consciousness.

"After all this, I won't start to hate you."

The next time I saw Sumire was two weeks later, on a Sunday, when I helped her move. She'd decided to move all of a sudden, and I was the only one who came to help. Other than books, she owned very little, and the whole procedure was over before we knew it. One good thing about being poor, at least.

I borrowed a friend's Toyota minivan and transported her things over to her new place in Yoyogi-Uehara. The apartment wasn't so new or much to look at, but compared to her old wooden building in Kichijoji – a place that should be on a list of designated historical sites – it was definitely a step up. An estate agent friend of Miu's had located the place for her; despite its convenient location, the rent was reasonable and it boasted a nice view. It was also twice as big as the old place. Definitely worth the move. Yoyogi Park was nearby, and she could walk to work if the mood took her.

"Starting next month I'll be working five days a week," she said. "Three days a week seems neither here nor there, and it's easier to stand commuting if you do it every day.

I have to pay more rent now, and Miu told me it'd be better all around if I became a full-time employee. I mean, if I stay at home, I still won't be able to write."

"Sounds like a good idea," I commented.

"My life will get more organized if I work every day, and I probably won't be calling you up at 3.30 in the morning. One good point about it."

"One *very* good point," I said. "But it's sad to think you'll be living so far away from me."

"You really feel that way?"

"Of course. Want me to rip out my heart and show you?"

I was sitting on the bare floor of the new apartment, leaning against the wall. Sumire was so bereft of household goods the new place looked deserted. There weren't any curtains in the windows, and the books that didn't fit into the bookshelf lay piled on the floor like a gang of intellectual refugees. The full-length mirror on the wall, a moving present from Miu, was the only thing that stood out. The caws of crows filtered in from the park on the twilight breeze. Sumire sat down next to me. "You know what?" she said.

"What?"

"If I were some good-for-nothing lesbian, would you still be my friend?"

"Whether you're a good-for-nothing lesbian or not doesn't matter. Imagine *The Greatest Hits of Bobby Darin* minus 'Mack the Knife'. That's what my life would be like without you."

Sumire narrowed her eyes and looked at me. "I'm not sure I follow your metaphor, but what you mean is you'd feel really lonely?"

"That's about the size of it," I said.

Sumire rested her head on my shoulder. Her hair was held back by a small hairclip, and I could see her small, nicely formed ears. Ears so pretty you'd think they had just been created. Soft, easily injured ears. I could feel her breath on my skin. She wore a pair of pink shorts and a faded, plain navy-blue T-shirt. The outline of her small nipples showed through the shirt. There was a faint odour of sweat. Her sweat and mine, the two odours subtly combined.

I wanted to hold her so badly. I was seized by a violent desire to push her down on the floor right then and there. But I knew it would be wasted effort. Suddenly I found it hard to breathe, and my field of vision narrowed. Time had lost an exit and spun its wheels. Desire swelled up in my trousers, hard as a rock. I was confused, bewildered. I tried to get a grip. I breathed in a lungful of fresh air, closed my eyes, and in that incomprehensible darkness I slowly began counting. My urges were so overpowering that tears came to my eyes.

"I like you, too," Sumire said. "In this whole big world, more than anyone else."

"After Miu, you mean," I said.

"Miu's a little different."

"How so?"

"The feelings I have for her are different from how I feel about you. What I mean is . . . hmm. How should I put it?"

"We good-for-nothing heterosexuals have a term for it," I said. "We say you get a hard-on."

Sumire laughed. "Other than wanting to be a novelist, I've never wanted anything so much. I've always been satisfied with exactly what I have. But now, right at this moment, I want Miu. Very, very much. I want to have her. Make her mine. I just *have* to. There are no other choices. Not one. I have no idea why things worked out like this. Does that . . . make sense?"

I nodded. My penis still maintained its overpowering rigidity, and I prayed that Sumire wouldn't notice.

"There's a great line by Groucho Marx," I said. "'She's so in love with me she doesn't know anything. That's why she's in love with me.'"

Sumire laughed.

"I hope things work out," I said. "But try your best to stay alert. You're still vulnerable. Remember that."

Without a word, Sumire took my hand and gently squeezed it. Her small, soft hand had a faint sheen of sweat. I imagined her hand stroking my rock-hard penis. I tried not to think that, but couldn't help it. As Sumire had said, there were no other choices. I imagined taking off her T-shirt, her shorts, her panties. Feeling her tight, taut nipples under my tongue. Spreading her legs wide, entering that wetness. Slowly, into the deep darkness within. It enticed me inside, enfolded me, then pushed me out . . . The illusion grabbed me and wouldn't let go. I closed my eyes tight again and let a concentrated clump of time wash over me. My face turned down, I waited patiently for the overheated air to blow above me and away.

"Why don't we have dinner together?" she asked. But I had to take the minivan I borrowed back to Hino by the end of the day. More than anything else, though, I had to be alone with my violent urges. I didn't want Sumire to get involved any more than she already was. I didn't know how far I could control myself if she was beside me. Past the point of no return, and I might completely lose it.

"Well, let me treat you to a nice dinner sometime soon, then. Tablecloths, wine. The works. Maybe next week," Sumire promised as we said goodbye. "Keep your diary free for me next week."

"Okay," I said.

I glanced at the full-length mirror as I passed by and saw my face. It had a strange expression. It was my face, all right, but where did that look come from? I didn't feel like retracing my steps and investigating further.

Sumire stood at the entrance to her new place to see me off. She waved goodbye, something she rarely did.

In the end, like so many beautiful promises in our lives, that dinner date never came to be. At the beginning of August I received a long letter from her.

6

The envelope had a large, colourful Italian stamp on it and was postmarked Rome, though I couldn't make out when it had been sent.

The day the letter arrived, I'd gone out to Shinjuku for the first time in quite a while, picked up a couple of new books at the Kinokuniya bookshop, and taken in a Luc Besson movie. Afterwards I stopped by a beer hall and enjoyed an anchovy pizza and a mug of dark beer. Only just beating the rush hour, I boarded the Chuo Line and read one of my new books until I arrived home at Kunitachi. I planned to make a simple dinner and watch a football match on TV. The ideal way to spend a summer holiday. Hot, alone, and free, not bothering anyone, and nobody bothering me.

When I got back home, there was a letter on the mat. The sender's name wasn't on the envelope, but one glance at the handwriting told me it was from Sumire. Hiero-glyphic writing, compact, hard, uncompromising. Writing that reminded me of the beetles they discovered inside the pyramids of Egypt. Like it's going to start crawling and disappear back into the darkness of history.

Rome?

I put the food I'd bought at a supermarket in the fridge and poured myself a tall glass of iced tea. I sat down in a chair in the kitchen, slit open the envelope with a paring knife, and read the letter. Five pages of stationery from the Rome Excelsior Hotel, crammed full of tiny writing in blue ink. Must have taken a lot of time to write that much. On the last page, in one corner, was some sort of stain – coffee, perhaps.

How are you?

I can imagine how surprised you must be to all of a sudden get a letter from me from Rome. You're so cool, though, it'd probably take more than Rome to surprise you. Rome's a bit too touristy. It'd have to be some place like Greenland, Timbuktu, or the Strait of Magellan, wouldn't it? Though I can tell you *I* find it hard to believe that here I am in Rome.

Anyway, I'm sorry I wasn't able to take you out to dinner like we planned. This Europe trip came right out of the blue, just after I moved. Then it was utter madness for a few days – running out to apply for a passport, buying suitcases, finishing up some work I'd begun. I'm not very good at remembering things – I don't need to tell *you*, do I? – but I do try my best to keep my promises. The ones I remember, that is.

Which is why I want to apologize for not keeping our dinner date.

I really enjoy my new apartment. Moving is certainly a pain (I know you did most of the work, for which I'm grateful; still, it's a pain), but once you're all moved in it's pretty nice. There're no roosters crowing in my new place, as in Kichijoji, instead a lot of crows making a racket like some old wailing women. At dawn flocks of them assemble in Yoyogi Park, and make such a ruckus you'd think the world was about to end. No need for an alarm clock, since the racket always wakes me up. Thanks to which I'm now like you, living an early-to-bed-early-to-rise farmer's lifestyle. I'm beginning to understand how it feels to have someone call you at 3.30 in the morning. *Beginning* to understand, mind you.

I'm writing this letter at an outdoor café on a side street in Rome, sipping espresso as thick as the devil's sweat, and I have this strange feeling that I'm not *myself* any more. It's hard to put it into words, but I guess it's as if I was fast asleep, and someone came, disassembled me, and hurriedly put me back together again. That sort of feeling. Can you understand what I'm getting at?

My eyes tell me I'm the same old me, but something's *different* from usual. Not that I can clearly recall what "usual" was. Ever since I stepped off the plane I can't shake this very real, deconstructive illusion. *Illusion?* I guess that's the word . . .

Sitting here, asking myself, "Why am I in Rome of all places?" everything around me starts to look unreal. Of course if I trace the details of how I got here I can come up with an explanation, but on a gut level I'm still not convinced. The me sitting here and the image of me I have are out of sync. To put it another way, I don't particularly *need* to be here, but nonetheless here I am. I know I'm being vague, but you understand me, don't you?

There's one thing I *can* say for sure: I wish you were here with me. Even though I have Miu with me, I'm lonely being so far away from you. If we were even farther apart, I know I'd feel even more lonely. I'd like to think you feel the same way.

So anyway, here Miu and I are, traipsing around Europe. She had some business to take care of and was planning originally to go around Italy and France by herself for two weeks, but asked me to come along as her personal secretary. She just blurted this out one morning, took me completely by surprise. My title might be "personal secretary", but I don't think I'm much use to her; still, the experience will do me good, and Miu tells me the trip's her present to me for stopping smoking. So all the agony I went through paid off in the end.

We landed first in Milan, went sightseeing, then rented a blue Alfa Romeo and headed south on the autostrada. We went around a few vineyards in Tuscany, and after taking care of business stayed a few nights in a charming little hotel, and then arrived in Rome. Business is always conducted in either English or French, so I don't have much of a role to play, though my Italian has come in handy in day-to-day things as we travel. If we went to Spain (which unfortunately won't happen on this trip), I might be of more use to Miu.

The Alfa Romeo we rented was a manual drive, so I was no help at all. Miu did all the driving. She can drive for hours and never seems to mind. Tuscany is all hills and curves, and it was amazing how smoothly she shifted gears up and down; watching her made me (and I'm not joking here) shiver all over. Being away from Japan, and simply being by her side are quite enough to satisfy me. If only we could stay this way for ever.

Next time I'll write about all the wonderful meals and wine we've had in Italy; it'd take too much time to do so now. In Milan we walked from store to store shopping. Dresses, shoes, underwear. Other than some pyjamas (I'd forgotten to take mine), I didn't buy anything. I didn't have much money, and besides there were so many beautiful things I had no idea where to start. That's the situation where my sense of judgement blows a fuse. Just being with Miu as she shopped was sufficient. She's an absolute master shopper, choosing only the most exquisite things, and buying only a select few. Like taking a bite of the tastiest part of a dish. Very smart and charming. When I watched her select some expensive silk stockings and underwear I found it hard to breathe. Drops of sweat bubbled up on my forehead. Which is pretty strange when you think about it.

I'm a girl, after all. I guess that's enough about shopping – writing about all that as well will make this too long.

At hotels we stay in separate rooms. Miu seems very insistent on this. Only once, in Florence, when our reservation got messed up somehow, did we end up having to share a room. It had twin beds, but just being able to sleep in the same room with her made my heart leap. I caught a glimpse of her coming out of the bath with a towel wrapped around her, and of her changing her clothes. Naturally I pretended not to look and read my book, but I did manage a peek. Miu has a truly gorgeous figure. She wasn't completely nude, but wore some tiny underwear; still her body was enough to take my breath away. Very slim, tight buns, a thoroughly attractive woman. I wish you could have seen it – though it's a little weird for me to say that.

I imagined being held by that lithe, slim body. All sorts of obscene images came to mind of us as I lay in bed in the same room with her, and I felt these thoughts gradually pushing me to some other place. I think I got a little too worked up – my period started that same night, way ahead of schedule. What a pain *that* was. Hmm. I know telling you this isn't going to get me anywhere. But I'll go ahead anyway – just to get the facts down on paper.

Last night we attended a concert in Rome. I wasn't expecting much, it being the off-season, but we managed to enjoy an incredible performance. Martha Argerich playing Liszt's Piano Concerto No. 1. I adore that piece. The conductor was Giuseppe Sinopoli. What a performance! Can't get bored when you listen to that kind of music – it was absolutely the most expansive, fantastic music I've ever heard. Come to think of it, maybe it was a bit *too* perfect for my taste. Liszt needs to be a bit slippery, and furtive – like music at a village festival. Take out the difficult parts and let me feel the *thrill* – that's what I like. Miu and I agreed on this point. There's a Vivaldi festival in Venice, and we're talking about going. Like when you and I talk about literature, Miu and I can talk about music till the cows come home.

This letter's getting pretty long, isn't it? It's like once I take hold of a pen and start to write I can't stop halfway. I've always been like that. They say well brought up girls don't overstay their welcome, but when it comes to writing (maybe not just writing?) my manners are hopeless. The waiter, with his white jacket, sometimes looks over at me with this disgusted look on his face. But even my hand gets tired, I'll admit. Besides, I've run out of paper.

Miu is out visiting an old friend in Rome, and I wandered the streets near the hotel, then decided to take a break in this café I came across, and here I am busily writing away to you. Like I'm on a desert island and I'm sending out a message in a bottle.

Strange thing is, when I'm not with Miu I don't feel like going anywhere. I've come all this way to Rome (and most likely won't come back again), but I just can't rouse myself to get up and see those ruins – what do they call those? – or those famous fountains. Or even to go shopping. It's enough just to sit here in a café, sniff the smell of the city, like a dog might, listen to voices and sounds, and gaze at the faces of the people passing by.

And suddenly I just got the feeling, while writing this letter to you, that what I described in the beginning – the strange sense of being disassembled – is starting to fade. It doesn't bother me so much now. It's like the way I feel when I've called you up in the middle of the night and just finished the call and stepped out of the phone box. Maybe you have that kind of effect on me?

What do you think? At any rate, please pray for my happiness and good fortune. I need your prayers.

Bye for now.

P.S. I'll probably be back home around the 15th of August. Then we can have dinner together – I promise! – before the summer's over.

Five days later a second letter came, posted from some obscure French village. A shorter letter than the first one. Miu and Sumire had left their rental car in Rome and taken a train to Venice. There they listened to two full days of Vivaldi. Most of the concerts were held at the church where Vivaldi had served as a priest. "If I don't hear any more Vivaldi for six months that's fine by me," wrote Sumire. Her descriptions of how delicious the paper-wrapped grilled seafood was in Venice were so realistic it made me want to dash off to Venice to try some for myself.

After Venice they returned to Milan, then flew to Paris. They took a break there, shopping some more, then boarded a train to Burgundy. One of Miu's good friends owned a huge house, a manor really, where they stayed. As in Italy, Miu made the rounds of several small vineyards on business. On free afternoons they took a picnic-basket lunch and went walking in the woods nearby. With a couple of bottles of wine to complement the meal, of course. "The wine here is simply out of this world," Sumire wrote.

Somehow, though, it looks like our original plan of returning to Japan on the 15th of August is going to change. After our work is done in France we may be taking a short holiday on a Greek island. This English gentleman we happened to meet here – a real gentleman, mind you – owns a villa on the island and invited us to use it for as long as we like. Great news! Miu likes the idea, too. We need a break from work, some time to just kick back and relax. The two of us lying on the pure white beaches of the Aegean, two beautiful sets of breasts pointed towards the sun, sipping wine with a scent of pine resin in it, just watching the clouds drift by. Doesn't that sound wonderful?

It certainly does, I thought.

That afternoon I went to the public pool and paddled

around, stopped in a nicely air-conditioned coffee shop on the way home, and read for an hour. When I got back to my place I listened to both sides of an old Ten Years After LP while ironing three shirts. Ironing done, I drank some cheap wine I'd got on sale, mixed with Perrier, and watched a football match I'd videotaped. Every time I saw a pass I thought I wouldn't have made myself, I shook my head and sighed. Judging the mistakes of strangers is an easy thing to do – and it feels pretty good.

After the football match I sank back in my chair, stared at the ceiling, and imagined Sumire in her village in France. By now she was already on that Greek island. Lying on the beach, gazing at the passing clouds. Either way, she was a long way from me. Rome, Greece, Timbuktu, Aruanda – it didn't matter. She was far, far away. And most likely that was the future in a nutshell, Sumire growing ever more distant. It made me sad. I felt like I was some meaningless bug clinging for no special reason to a high stone wall on a windy night, with no plans, no beliefs. Sumire said she missed me. But she had Miu beside her. I had no one. All I had was – me. Same as always.

Sumire didn't come back on 15 August. Her phone still just had a curt *I'm-away-on-a-trip* recording on it. One of her first purchases after she moved was a phone with an answering machine, so she wouldn't have to go out on rainy nights, umbrella in hand, to a phone box. An excellent idea all round. I didn't leave a message.

I called her again on the 18th but got the same recording. After the lifeless beep I left my name and a simple message for her to call me when she got back. Most likely she and Miu found their Greek island too much fun to want to leave.

In the interval between my two calls I coached one football practice at my school and slept once with my girlfriend. She was well tanned, having just returned from a holiday in Bali with her husband and two children. As I held her I thought of Sumire on her Greek island. Inside her, I couldn't help but imagine Sumire's body.

If I hadn't known Sumire I could have easily fallen for this woman, seven years my senior (and whose son was one of my students). She was a beautiful, energetic, kind woman. She wore a bit too much make-up for my liking, but dressed nicely. She worried about being a little overweight, but shouldn't have. I certainly wasn't about to complain about her sexy figure. She knew all my desires, everything I wanted and didn't want. She knew just how far to go and when to stop – in bed and out. Made me feel like I was flying first class.

"I haven't slept with my husband for almost a year," she revealed to me as she lay in my arms. "You're the only one."

But I couldn't love her. For whatever reason, that unconditional, natural intimacy Sumire and I had just wasn't there. A thin, transparent veil always came between us. Visible or not, a barrier remained. Awkward silences came on us all the time – particularly when we said goodbye. That never happened with me and Sumire. Being with this woman confirmed one undeniable fact: I needed Sumire more than ever.

After the woman left, I went for a walk alone, wandered

aimlessly for a while, then dropped by a bar near the station and had a Canadian Club on the rocks. As always at times like those, I felt like the most wretched person alive. I quickly drained my first drink and ordered another, closed my eyes and thought of Sumire. Sumire, topless, sunbathing on the white sands of a Greek island. At the table next to mine four college boys and girls were drinking beer, laughing, and having a good time. An old number by Huey Lewis and the News was playing. I could smell pizza baking.

When did my youth slip away from me? I suddenly thought. It *was* over, wasn't it? Seemed just like yesterday I was still only half grown up. Huey Lewis and the News had a couple of hit songs then. Not so many years ago. And now here I was, inside a closed circuit, spinning my wheels. Knowing I wasn't getting anywhere, but spinning just the same. I had to. Had to keep that up or I wouldn't be able to survive.

That night I got a phone call from Greece. At 2 a.m.

But it wasn't Sumire. It was Miu.

7

The first thing I heard was a man's deep voice in heavily
accented English, spouting my name and then shouting,
"I've reached the right person, yes?" I'd been fast asleep. My
mind was a blank, a rice paddy in the middle of a rainstorm,
and I couldn't work out what was going on. The bed sheets
still retained a faint memory of the afternoon's lovemaking,
and reality was one step out of line, a cardigan with the
buttons done up wrong. The man spoke my name again.
"I've reached the right person, yes?"

"Yes, you have," I replied. It didn't sound like my name,
but there it was. For a while there was a crackle of static,
as if two different air masses had collided. Must be Sumire
making an overseas call from Greece, I imagined. I held
the receiver away from my ear a bit, waiting for her voice
to come on. But the voice I heard next wasn't Sumire's,
but Miu's.

"I'm sure you've heard about me from Sumire?"

"Yes, I have," I answered.

Her voice on the phone line was distorted by some far-off, inorganic substance, but I could still sense the tension in it. Something rigid and hard flowed through the phone like clouds of dry ice and into my room, throwing me wide awake. I sat bolt upright in bed and adjusted my grip on the receiver.

"I have to talk quickly," said Miu breathlessly. "I'm calling from a Greek island, and it's next to impossible to get through to Tokyo – even when you do they cut you off. I tried so many times, and finally got through. So I'm going to skip formalities and get right to the point, if you don't mind?"

"I don't mind," I said.

"Can you come here?"

"By here, you mean Greece?"

"Yes. As soon as you possibly can."

I blurted out the first thing that came to mind. "Did something happen to Sumire?"

A pause as Miu took in a breath. "I still don't know. But I think she would want you to come here. I'm certain of it."

"You *think* she would?"

"I can't go into it over the phone. There's no telling when we'll be cut off, and besides, it's a delicate sort of problem, and I'd much rather talk to you face to face. I'll pay the return fare. Just come. The sooner the better. Just buy a ticket. First class, whatever you like."

The new term at school began in ten days. I'd have to be back before then, but if I wanted to, a round trip to Greece wasn't beyond the realm of possibility. I was scheduled to go to school twice during the break to take care of some business, but I should be able to have somebody cover for me.

"I'm pretty sure I can come," I said. "Yes, I think I can. But where exactly is it I'm supposed to go?"

She told me the name of the island. I wrote down what she said on the inside cover of a book next to my bed. It sounded vaguely familiar.

"You take a plane from Athens to Rhodes, then take a ferry. There are two ferries a day to the island, one in the morning and one in the evening. I'll go down to the harbour whenever the ferries arrive. Will you come?"

"I think I'll make it somehow. It's just that I – " I started to say, and the line went dead. Suddenly, violently, like someone taking an axe to a rope. And again that awful static. Thinking we might be connected again, I sat there for a minute, phone against my ear, waiting, but all I heard was that grating noise. I hung up the phone and got out of bed. In the kitchen I had a glass of cold barley tea and leaned back against the fridge, trying to gather my thoughts.

Was I really going to get on a plane and fly all the way to Greece?

The answer was yes. I had no other choice.

I pulled a large world atlas down from my bookshelf to locate the island Miu had told me about. It was near Rhodes, she'd said, but it was no easy task to find it among the myriad islands that dotted the Aegean. Finally, though, I was able to spot, in tiny print, the name of the place I was looking for. A small island near the Turkish border. So small you couldn't really tell its shape.

I pulled my passport out of a drawer and checked it was

still valid. Next I gathered all the cash I had in the house and stuffed it in my wallet. It didn't amount to much, but I could withdraw more from the bank in the morning. I had some money in a savings account and had barely touched my summer bonus. That and my credit card and I should be able to come up with enough for a return ticket to Greece. I packed some clothes in a vinyl gym bag and tossed in a toilet kit. And two Joseph Conrad novels I'd been meaning to re-read. I hesitated about packing my swimming trunks, but ended up taking them. Maybe I'd get there and whatever problem there was would be solved, everybody healthy and happy, the sun hanging peacefully in the sky, and I'd enjoy a leisurely swim or two before I had to come home – which of course would be the best outcome for everyone involved.

Those things taken care of, I turned out the light, sunk my head back on the pillow, and tried to go back to sleep. It was just past three, and I could still catch a few winks before morning. But I couldn't sleep. Memories of that harsh static thrummed in my blood. Deep inside my head I could hear that man's voice, barking out my name. I switched on the light, got out of bed again, went to the kitchen, brewed some iced tea, and drank it. Then I replayed the entire conversation I'd had with Miu, every word in order. Her words were vague, abstract, full of ambiguities. But there were two facts in what she told me. I wrote them both down on a memo pad.

1. Something has happened to Sumire. But Miu doesn't know what it is.
2. I have to get there as soon as possible. Sumire, too, Miu thinks, wants me to do that.

I stared at the memo pad. And I underlined two phrases.

1. Something has happened to Sumire. But Miu
doesn't know what it is.
2. I have to get there as soon as possible. Sumire,
too, Miu thinks, wants me to do that.

I couldn't imagine what had happened to Sumire on that small Greek island. But I was sure it had to be something bad. The question was, *how* bad? Until morning there wasn't a thing I could do about it. I sat in my chair, feet up on the table, reading a book and waiting for the first light to show. It seemed to take forever.

At first light I boarded the Chuo Line to Shinjuku, hopped aboard the Narita Express, and arrived at the airport. At nine I made the rounds of airline ticket counters, only to learn that there weren't any direct flights between Narita and Athens. After a bit of trial and error I booked a business-class seat on the KLM flight to Amsterdam. I'd be able to change there onto a flight to Athens. Then at Athens I'd take an Olympic Airways domestic flight to Rhodes. The KLM people made all the arrangements. As long as no problems arose, I should be able to make the two connections okay. It was the fastest way to get there. I had an open ticket for the return flight, and I could come back any time in the next three months. I paid by credit card. Any bags to check in? they asked me. No, I replied.

I had time before my flight, so I ate breakfast at the airport restaurant. I withdrew some cash from an ATM and bought dollar traveller's cheques. Next I bought a guidebook to Greece in the bookshop. The name of the island Miu told me wasn't in the little book, but I did need to get some information about the country – the currency, the climate, the basics. Other than the history of ancient Greece and classical drama, there wasn't much I knew about the place. About as much as I knew of the geography of Jupiter or the inner workings of a Ferrari's cooling system. Not once in my life had I considered the possibility of going to Greece. At least not until 2 a.m. on that particular day.

Just before noon I phoned one of my fellow teachers. Something unfortunate happened to a relative of mine, I told her, I'll be away from Tokyo for about a week, so I wonder if you'd take care of things at school until I get back. No problem, she replied. We'd helped each other out like this a number of times, it was no big deal. "Where are you going?" she asked me. "Shikoku," I answered. I just couldn't very well tell her I was heading off to Greece.

"I'm sorry to hear that," she said. "Anyway, make sure you get back in time for the start of the new term. And pick up a souvenir for me if you can, okay?"

"Of course," I said. I'd work that one out later.

I went to the business-class lounge, lay back in a sofa, and dozed for a bit, an unsettled sleep. The world had lost all sense of reality. Colours were unnatural, details crude. The background was papier mâché, the stars made out of aluminium foil. You could see the glue and the heads of the nails holding it all together. Airport announcements flitted in and out of my consciousness. "All passengers on Air France flight 275, bound for Paris." In the midst of this illogical dream – or uncertain wakefulness – I thought about

Sumire. Like some documentary of ages past, fragments sprang to mind of the times and places we'd shared. In the bustle of the airport, passengers dashing here and there, the world I shared with Sumire seemed shabby, helpless, uncertain. Neither of us knew anything that really mattered, nor did we have the ability to rectify that. There was nothing solid we could depend on. We were almost boundless zeros, just pitiful little beings swept from one kind of oblivion to another.

I woke in an unpleasant sweat, my shirt plastered to my chest. My body was listless, my legs swollen. I felt as if I'd swallowed an overcast sky. I must have looked pale. One of the lounge staff asked me, worriedly, if I was okay. "I'm all right," I replied, "the heat's just getting to me." Would you like something cold to drink? she asked. I thought for a moment and asked for a beer. She brought me a chilled facecloth, a Heineken, and a bag of salted peanuts. After wiping my sweaty face and drinking half the beer, I felt better. And I could sleep a little.

The flight left Narita just about on time, taking the polar route to Amsterdam. I wanted to sleep some more, so I had a couple of whiskys and when I woke up, had a little dinner. I didn't have much of an appetite and skipped breakfast. I wanted to keep my mind a blank, so when I was awake I concentrated on reading Conrad.

In Amsterdam I changed planes, arrived in Athens, went to the domestic flight terminal, and, with barely a moment to spare, boarded the 727 bound for Rhodes. The plane was packed with an animated bunch of young people from every imaginable country. They were all tanned, dressed in T-shirts or tank tops and cut-off jeans. Most of the young men were growing beards (or maybe had forgotten to shave) and had dishevelled hair pulled back in ponytails. Dressed in beige slacks, a white short-sleeve polo shirt and dark-blue cotton jacket, I looked out of place. I'd even forgotten to bring any sunglasses. But who could blame me? Not too many hours before I had been in my apartment in Kunitachi, worrying about what I should do with my rubbish.

At Rhodes airport I asked at the information desk where I could catch the ferry to the island. It was at a harbour nearby. If I hurried, I might be able to make the evening ferry. "Isn't it sold out sometimes?" I asked, just to be sure. The pointy-nosed woman of indeterminate age at the information counter frowned and waved her hand dismissively. "They can always make room for one more," she replied. "It's not an elevator."

I hailed a taxi and headed to the harbour. "I'm in a hurry," I told the driver, but he didn't seem to catch my meaning. The cab didn't have any air-conditioning, and a hot, dusty wind blew in the open window. All the while the taxi driver, in rough, sweaty English, ran on and on with some gloomy diatribe about the Euro. I made polite noises to show I was following, but I wasn't really listening. Instead, I squinted at the bright Rhodes scenery passing by outside. The sky was cloudless, not a hint of rain. The sun baked the stone walls of the houses. A layer of dust covered the gnarled trees beside the road, and people sat in the shade of the trees or under open tents and gazed, almost silently, at the world. I began to wonder if I was in the right place. The gaudy signs in Greek letters, however, advertising cigarettes and ouzo and overflowing the road from the airport into town, told me that – sure enough – this was Greece.

The evening ferry was still in the port. It was bigger than I'd imagined. In the stern was a space for transporting cars, and two medium-sized lorries full of food and sundries and an old Peugeot sedan were already aboard, waiting for the ship to pull out of the port. I bought a ticket and got on, and I'd barely taken a seat on a deckchair when the line to the dock was untied and the engines roared into life. I sighed and looked up at the sky. All I could do now was wait for the ship to take me where I was going.

I removed my sweaty, dusty cotton jacket, folded it and stuffed it in my bag. It was 5 p.m., but the sun was still in the middle of the sky, the sunlight overpowering. The breeze blowing from the bow under the canvas awning wafted over me, and ever so slowly I began to feel calmer. The gloomy emotions that had swept through me in the lounge at Narita airport had disappeared. Though there was still a bitter aftertaste.

There were only a few tourists on board, so I guessed that the island I was heading for was not such a popular holiday spot. The vast majority of passengers were locals, mainly old people who'd taken care of business on Rhodes and were heading home. Their purchases lay carefully at their feet, like fragile animals. The old people's faces were all deeply etched with wrinkles and deadpan, as if the overpowering sun and a lifetime of hard work had robbed them of all expression.

There were also a few young soldiers on board. And two hippie travellers, heavy-looking backpacks in hand, sitting on the deck. Both with skinny legs and grim faces.

There was a teenage Greek girl, too, in a long skirt. She was lovely, with deep, dark eyes. Her long hair blew in the breeze as she chatted to her girlfriend. A gentle smile played around the corners of her mouth, as if something wonderful was about to occur. Her gold earrings glinted brightly in the sun. The young soldiers leaned against the deck railing, smoking, looking cool, throwing a quick glance in the girl's direction from time to time.

I sipped a lemon soda I'd bought at the ferry's canteen and gazed at the deep blue sea and the tiny islands floating by. Most were not so much islands as crags in the sea, completely deserted. White seabirds rested on the tip of the rocks, scanning the ocean for fish. They ignored our ship. Waves broke at the foot of the cliffs, creating a dazzling white border. Occasionally I spotted an inhabited island. Tough-looking trees grew all over it, and white-walled houses dotted the slopes. Brightly coloured boats bobbed in the inlet, their tall masts inscribing arcs as they rolled with the waves.

A wrinkled old man sitting next to me offered me a cigarette. Thank you, I smiled, waving my hand, but I don't smoke. He proffered a stick of spearmint gum instead. I took it gratefully, and continued to gaze out to sea as I chewed.

It was after seven when the ferry reached the island. The blazing sun had passed its zenith, but the sky was as light as before, the summer light actually increasing in brilliance. As if on some huge nameplate, the name of the island was written in gigantic letters on the white walls of a building in the harbour. The ferry sidled up to the wharf, and one by one the passengers walked down the gangplank, luggage in hand. An open-air café faced the harbour, and people who'd come to meet the ship waited there until they recognized the people they were looking for.

As soon as I debarked I looked around for Miu. But there was no one around who might be her. Several owners of inns came up, asking me if I was looking for a place to stay for the night. "No, I'm not," I said each time, shaking my head. Even so, each one handed me a card before leaving.

The people who'd left the ship with me scattered in all directions. Shoppers trudged home, travellers went off to hotels and inns. As soon as the people who'd come to greet their returning friends spotted them, they hugged each other tightly or shook hands, and off they'd go. The two lorries and the Peugeot, too, were unloaded and roared off into the distance. Even the cats and dogs that had assembled out of curiosity were gone before long. The only ones left were a group of sunburned old folks with time on their hands. And me, gym bag in hand, thoroughly out of place.

I took a seat at the café and ordered an iced tea, wondering what I should do next. There wasn't much I could do. Night was fast approaching, and I knew nothing about the island and the layout of the land. If nobody came after a while, I'd get a room somewhere and the next morning come back to the harbour, hopefully to meet with Miu. According to Sumire, Miu was a methodical woman, so I couldn't believe she'd stand me up. If she couldn't make it to the harbour, there must be some very good explanation. Maybe she didn't think I'd get here so quickly.

I was starving. A feeling of such extreme hunger I felt sure you could see through me. All the fresh sea air must have made my body realize it hadn't had any nourishment since morning. I didn't want to miss Miu, though, so I decided to wait some more in the café. Every so often a local would pass by and give me a curious glance.

At the kiosk next to the café I bought a small English pamphlet about the history and geography of the island. I leafed through it as I sipped the incredibly tasteless iced tea. The island's population ranged from 3,000 to 6,000, depending on the season. The population went up in the summer with the number of tourists, down in winter when people went elsewhere in search of work. The island had no industry to speak of, and agriculture was pretty limited – olives and a couple of varieties of fruit. And there was fishing and sponge-diving. Which is why, since the beginning of the twentieth century, most of the islanders had emigrated to America. The majority moved to Florida, where they could put their fishing and sponging skills to good use. There was even a town in Florida with the same name as the island.

On top of the hills was a military radar installation. Near the civilian harbour was a second, smaller harbour where military patrol ships docked. With the Turkish border nearby, the Greeks wanted to prevent illegal border crossings and smuggling, which is why there were soldiers in the town. Whenever there was a dispute with Turkey – in fact small-scale skirmishes often broke out – traffic in and out of the harbour picked up.

More than 2,000 years ago, when Greek civilization was at its peak, this island, situated along the main route to

Asia, flourished as a trading centre. Back then the hills were still covered with green trees, put to good use by the thriving ship-building industry. When Greek civilization declined, though, and all the trees had been cut down (an abundant greenery never to return again), the island quickly slid downhill economically. Finally, the Turks came in. Their rule was draconian, according to the pamphlet. If something wasn't to their liking, they'd lop off people's ears and noses as easily as pruning trees. At the end of the nineteenth century, after countless bloody battles, the island finally won its independence from Turkey, and the blue-and-white Greek flag fluttered over the harbour. Next came Hitler. The Germans built a radar and weather station on top of the hills to monitor the nearby sea, since the hills provided the best possible view. An English bombing force from Malta bombed the station. It bombed the harbour as well as the hilltop, sinking a number of innocent fishing boats and killing some hapless fishermen. More Greeks died in the attack than did Germans, and some old-timers still bore a grudge over the incident.

Like most Greek islands there was little flat space here, it was mostly steep, unforgiving hills, with only one town along the shore, just south of the harbour. Far from the town was a beautiful, quiet beach, but to get to it you had to climb over a steep hill. The easily accessible places didn't have such nice beaches, which might be one reason the number of tourists remained static. There were some Greek Orthodox monasteries up in the hills, but the monks led strictly observant lives, and casual visitors weren't allowed.

As far as I could tell from reading the pamphlet, this was

a pretty typical Greek island. For some reason, though, Englishmen found the island particularly charming (the British *are* a bit eccentric) and, in their zeal for the place, built a colony of summer cottages on a rise near the harbour. In the late 1960s several British writers lived there and wrote their novels while gazing at the blue sea and the white clouds. Several of their works became critically acclaimed, resulting in the island garnering a reputation among the British literati as a romantic spot. As far as this notable aspect of their island's culture was concerned, though, the local Greek inhabitants couldn't have cared less.

I read all this to take my mind off how hungry I was. I closed the pamphlet and looked around me again. The old people in the café gazed unceasingly at the sea, as if they were contestants in a staring contest. It was already eight o'clock, and my hunger was turning into something close to physical pain. The smell of roast meat and grilled fish drifted over from somewhere and, like a good-natured torturer, seized me by the guts. I couldn't endure it any more and stood up. Just as I picked up my bag and was about to start searching for a restaurant, a woman silently appeared before me.

The sun, finally sinking into the sea, shone directly on the woman, her knee-length white skirt rippling slightly as she strode down the stone steps. She wore small tennis shoes, and her legs were girlish. She had on a sleeveless light-green blouse, a narrow-brimmed hat and carried a small cloth shoulder bag. The way she walked was so natural, so ordinary, she blended into the scenery, and at first I took her for a local. But she was heading straight for me, and as she approached I could make out her Asian features. Half reflexively I sat down, then stood up again. The woman removed her sunglasses and spoke my name.

"Sorry I'm so late," she said. "I had to go to the police station, and all the paperwork took a long time. And I never imagined you'd be here today. Tomorrow at noon at the earliest, I thought."

"I managed to make all my connections," I said. *The police station?*

Miu looked straight at me and smiled faintly. "If it's all right with you, why don't we go somewhere to eat and talk. I've only had breakfast today. How about you? Are you hungry?"

You'd better believe it, I replied.

She led me to a taverna on a side street near the harbour. There was a charcoal grill set up near the entrance and all kinds of fresh seafood cooking away on the iron grill. Do you like fish? Asked Miu, and I said I did. She spoke to the waiter, ordering in broken Greek. First he brought a carafe of white wine, bread, and olives. Without any toasts or further ado, we poured ourselves some wine and started drinking. I ate some of the coarse bread and a few olives to ease my hunger pangs.

Miu was beautiful. My first impression was of that clear and simple fact. No, maybe it wasn't that clear or that simple. Maybe I was under some terrible mistaken impression. Maybe for some reason I'd been swallowed up in some other person's unalterable dream. Thinking about it now, I can't rule out that possibility. All I can say for sure

101

is that at that moment I saw her as an extremely lovely woman.

She wore several rings on her slim fingers. One was a simple gold wedding band. While I tried hurriedly to arrange my first impressions of her in some kind of order, she gazed at me with gentle eyes, taking an occasional sip of wine.

"I feel like I've met you before," she said. "Perhaps because I hear about you all the time."

"Sumire's told me a lot about you, too," I said.

Miu beamed. When she smiled, and then only, charming small lines appeared at the corners of her eyes. "I guess we can forgo introductions, then."

I nodded.

What I liked most about Miu was that she didn't try to hide her age. According to Sumire, she must be 38 or 39. And indeed she looked that age. With her slim, tight figure, a little make-up and she'd easily pass for late twenties. But she didn't make the effort. Miu let age naturally rise to the surface, accepted it for what it was, and made her peace with it.

Miu popped an olive into her mouth, grasped the pit with her fingers and, like a poet getting the punctuation just right, gracefully discarded it in an ashtray.

"I'm sorry to call you up like that in the middle of the night," she said. "I wish I could have explained things better then, but I was too upset and didn't know where to begin. I'm still not totally calm, but my initial confusion has settled a bit."

"What in the world happened?" I asked.

Miu brought her hands together on the table, separated

them, brought them together again.

"Sumire has disappeared."

"*Disappeared?*"

"Like smoke," Miu said. She took a sip of wine.

She continued. "It's a long story, so I think I'd better start at the beginning and tell it in the right order. Otherwise some of the nuances might not come through. The story itself is quite subtle. But let's eat first. It's not like each second counts right now, and it's hard to think straight if you're hungry. Also, it's a bit too noisy to talk here."

The restaurant was filled with Greeks gesturing and talking boisterously. So that we didn't have to shout at each other, Miu and I leaned forward across the table, our heads close together as we talked. Presently the waiter brought over a heaping plate of Greek salad and a large grilled whitefish. Miu sprinkled some salt on the fish, squeezed out half a lemon, and dripped some olive oil onto her portion. I did the same. We concentrated on eating for a while. As she said, first things first. We needed to assuage our hunger.

How long could I stay here? she asked. "The new term begins in a week," I replied, "so I have to be back by then. Otherwise things will be a bit sticky." Miu gave a matter-of-fact nod. She pursed her lips and seemed to be working out something. She didn't say anything predictable, like "Don't worry, you'll be back by then," or "I wonder if things'll be all settled by then." She came to her own private conclusion, which she tucked away in a drawer, and silently went back to her meal.

After dinner, as we were having coffee, she broached the subject of the air fare. Would you mind taking the amount in dollar traveller's cheques? she asked. Or else I could have the money transferred to your account in yen after you return to Tokyo. Which do you prefer? I'm not strapped for funds, I answered, I can pay it myself. But Miu insisted on paying. I'm the one who asked you to come, she said.

I shook my head. "It's not like I'm being polite or anything. A little bit later on, and I probably would have come here of my own accord. That's what I'm trying to say."

Miu gave it some thought and nodded. "I am very grateful to you. For coming here. I can't tell you how much."

When we left the restaurant, the sky was a brilliant splash of colours. The kind of air that felt like if you breathed it in, your lungs would be dyed the same shade of blue. Tiny stars began to twinkle. Barely able to wait for the long summer day to be over, the locals were out for an after-dinner stroll around the harbour. Families, couples, groups of friends. The gentle scent of the tide at the end of the day enveloped the streets. Miu and I walked through the town. The right side of the street was lined with shops, small hotels, and restaurants with tables set up on the pavement. Cosy yellow lights shone at small, wooden-shuttered windows, and Greek music filtered down from a radio. On the left side the sea spread out, dark waves placidly breaking on the wharves.

"In a while the road goes uphill," Miu said. "We can either take some steep stairs or a gentle slope. The stairs are faster. Do you mind?"

"No, I don't," I answered.

Narrow stone stairs paralleled the slope of the hill. They were long and steep, but Miu's trainer-clad feet showed no signs of tiring, and she never slackened her pace. The hem of her skirt just in front of me swished pleasantly from side to side, her tanned, shapely calves shone in the light of the almost full moon. I got winded first and had to stop to take some deep breaths. As we made our way up, the lights of the harbour became smaller and further away. All the activities of the people who'd been right beside me were absorbed into that anonymous line of lights. It was an impressive sight, something I wanted to cut out with scissors and pin to the wall of my memory.

The place where Miu and Sumire were staying was a small cottage with a veranda facing the sea. White walls and a red-tiled roof, the door painted a deep green. A riot of red bougainvilleas overgrew the low stone wall that surrounded the house. She opened the unlocked door and invited me in.

The cottage was pleasantly cool. There was a living room and a medium-sized dining room and kitchen. The walls were white stucco, with a couple of abstract paintings. In the living room there was a sofa and bookshelf, and a compact stereo. Two bedrooms and a small but clean-looking tiled bathroom. None of the furniture was very appealing, just cosy and lived in.

Miu took off her hat and laid her bag down on the kitchen worktop. "Would you like something to drink?" she asked. "Or would you like a shower first?"

"Think I'll take a shower first," I said.

I washed my hair and shaved. Blow-dried my hair and changed into a fresh T-shirt and shorts. Made me feel halfway back to normal. Below the mirror in the bathroom there were two toothbrushes, one blue, the other red. I wondered which was Sumire's.

I went back into the living room and found Miu in an easy chair, brandy glass in hand. She invited me to join her, but what I really wanted was a cold beer. I got an Amstel beer from the fridge and poured it into a tall glass. Sunk deep in her chair, Miu was quiet for a long time. It didn't look like she was trying to find the right words she wanted to say, rather that she was immersed in some personal memory, one without beginning and without end.

"How long have you been here?" I ventured.

"Today is the eighth day," Miu said after thinking about it.

"And Sumire disappeared from here?"

"That's right. Like I said before, just like smoke."

"When did this happen?"

"At night, four days ago," she said, looking around the room as if seeking a clue. "I don't know where to begin."

"Sumire told me in her letters about going to Paris from Milan," I said. "Then about taking the train to Burgundy. You stayed at your friend's large estate house in a Burgundy village."

"Well, then, I'll pick up the story from there," she said.

8

"I've known the wine producers around that village for ages, and I know their wines like I know the layout of my own house. What kind of wine the grapes on a certain slope in a certain field will produce. How that year's weather affects the flavour, which producers are working hardest, whose son is trying his best to help his father. How much in loans certain producers have taken out, who's bought a new Citroën. Those kinds of things. Wine is like breeding thoroughbreds – you have to know the lineage and the latest information. You can't do business based just on what tastes good and what doesn't."

Miu stopped for a moment to catch her breath. She seemed unable to decide whether to go on or not. She continued.

"There are a couple of places in Europe I buy from, but that village in Burgundy is my main supplier. So I try to spend a fair amount of time there at least once a year, to renew old friendships and gather the latest news. I always go alone, but this time we were visiting Italy first, and I decided to take Sumire with me. It's more convenient sometimes to have another person with you on trips like this, and besides, I'd had her study Italian. In the end I decided I *would* rather go alone and planned to make up some excuse to have her go back home before I set out for France. I've been used to travelling alone ever since I was young, and no matter how close you are to them it's not easy to be with someone else day after day.

"Sumire was surprisingly capable and took care of lots of details for me. Buying tickets, making hotel reservations, negotiating prices, keeping expense records, searching out good local restaurants. Those kinds of things. Her Italian was much improved, and I liked her healthy curiosity, which helped me experience things I never would have if I'd been alone. I was surprised at how easy it is to be with someone else. I felt that way, I think, because of something special that brought us together."

"I remember very well the first time we met and we talked about Sputniks. She was talking about Beatnik writers, and I mistook the word and said 'Sputnik'. We laughed about it, and that broke the ice. Do you know what 'Sputnik' means in Russian? 'Travelling companion'. I looked it up in a dictionary not long ago. Kind of a strange coincidence if you think about it. I wonder why the Russians gave their satellite that strange name. It's just a poor little lump of metal, spinning around the Earth."

Miu was silent for just a moment, then continued.

*

"Anyway, I ended up taking Sumire with me to Burgundy. While I was seeing old acquaintances and taking care of business, Sumire, whose French was nonexistent, borrowed the car and drove around the area. In one town she happened to meet a wealthy old Spanish lady, and they chatted in Spanish and got to be friends. The lady introduced Sumire to an Englishman who was staying in their hotel. He was more than 50, a writer of some sort, very refined and handsome. I'm positive he was gay. He had a secretary with him who seemed to be his boyfriend.

"They invited us for dinner. They were very nice people, and as we talked we realized we had some mutual acquaintances, and I felt like I'd found some kindred spirits.

"The Englishman told us he had a small cottage on an island in Greece and would be happy if we used it. He always used the cottage for a month in the summer, but this summer he had some work that kept him from going. Houses are best occupied, otherwise the caretakers will get lazy, he told us. So if it isn't any bother, please feel free to use it. This cottage, in other words."

Miu gazed around the room.

"When I was in college I visited Greece. It was one of those whirlwind tours where you leap from port to port, but still I fell in love with the country. That's why it was such an enticing offer to have a free house on a Greek island to use for as long as we wanted. Sumire jumped at the chance, too. I offered to pay a fair price to rent the cottage, but the Englishman refused, saying he wasn't in the rental business. We batted some ideas around for a while, and ended up agreeing that I would send a case of red wine to his home in London to thank him.

"Life on the island was like a dream. For the first time in I don't know how long I could enjoy a real holiday, without any schedule to worry about. Communications are a bit backward here – you know about the awful phone service – and there aren't any faxes or the Internet. Getting back to Tokyo later than originally planned would cause a bit of a problem for other people, but once I got here it didn't seem to matter any more.

"Sumire and I got up early every morning, packed a bag with towels, water, sunscreen, and walked to the beach on the other side of the mountains. The shore is so beautiful it takes your breath away. The sand is pure white, and there are hardly any waves. It's a little out of the way, though, and very few people go there, particularly in the morning. Everyone, men and women, swims nude. We did, too. It feels fantastic to swim in the pure blue sea in the morning, as bare as the day you were born. You feel like you're in another world.

"When we tired of swimming, Sumire and I would lie on the beach and get a tan. At first we were a little embarrassed to be nude in front of each other, but once we got used to it, it was no big deal. The energy of the place was working on us, I suppose. We'd spread sunscreen on each other's backs, loll in the sun, reading, dozing, just chatting. It made me feel truly free.

"We'd walk back home over the mountains, take showers and have a simple meal, then set off down the stairs to town. We'd have tea in a harbour café, read the English paper, buy some food in a shop, go home, then spend our time as we pleased until evening – reading out on the veranda or listening to music. Sometimes Sumire was in her room, writing apparently. I could hear her opening up her Power-Book and clattering away on the keys. In the evening we'd go out to the harbour to watch the ferryboat come in. We'd have a cool drink and watch the people getting off the ship.

"There we were, sitting quietly on the edge of the world, and no one could see us. That's the way it felt – like Sumire and I were the only ones here. There was nothing else we had to think about. I didn't want to move, didn't want to go anywhere. I just wanted to stay this way for ever. I knew that was impossible – our life here was just a momentary illusion, and someday reality would yank us back to the world we came from. But until that time came I wanted to enjoy each day to the fullest, without worrying about anything. We loved our life here. Until four days ago."

On their fourth morning there they went as usual to the beach, skinny-dipped, returned home, and left again for the harbour. The waiter at the café remembered them – the generous tips Miu always left didn't hurt – and greeted them warmly. He made some polite comment about how beautiful they looked. Sumire went to the kiosk and bought a copy of the English newspaper published in Athens. That was their only link with the outside world. Sumire's job was reading the paper. She'd check the exchange rate and translate and read aloud to Miu any major news item or interesting article she happened to come across.

The article Sumire picked to read aloud that particular day was a report of a 70-year-old lady who was eaten by her cats. It happened in a small suburb of Athens. The dead woman had lost her husband, a businessman, eleven years before and ever since had lived a quiet life in a two-room apartment with several cats as her only friends. One day the woman collapsed face down on her sofa from a heart attack and expired. It wasn't known how much time had elapsed between her attack and her death. At any rate, the woman's soul passed through all the set stages to bid farewell to its old companion, the body it had inhabited for 70 years. She didn't have any relatives or friends who visited her regularly, and her body wasn't discovered until a week later. The doors were shut, the windows shuttered, and the cats couldn't get out after the death of their owner. There wasn't any food in the apartment. There must have been something in the refrigerator, but cats don't possess the necessary skill to open fridge doors. Starving, they devoured the flesh of their owner.

Taking an occasional sip from her coffee cup, Sumire translated the article in stages. Some bees buzzed around the table, licking the jam a previous patron had spilled. Miu gazed at the sea through her sunglasses, listening intently to Sumire.

"And then what happened?" Miu asked.

"That's it," said Sumire, folding the tabloid in half and laying it on the table. "That's all the newspaper says."

"What could have happened to the cats?"

"I don't know . . ." Sumire said, pursing her lips to one side and giving it some thought. "Newspapers are all the same. They never tell you what you really want to know."

The bees, as if sensing something, flew up in the air and with a ceremonious buzz circled for a while, then settled again on the table. They returned to their jam licking.

"And what was the fate of the cats, one wonders," Sumire said, tugging at the collar of her oversize T-shirt and smoothing out the wrinkles. She had on a T-shirt and shorts and – Miu happened to know – no underwear underneath. "Cats that develop a taste for human flesh might turn into man-eating cats, so maybe they destroyed them. Or maybe the police said, 'Hey, you guys have suffered enough,' and they were acquitted."

"If you were the mayor or chief of police in that town, what would you do?"

Sumire thought about it. "How about placing them in an institution and reforming them? Turn them into vegetarians."

"Not a bad idea." Miu laughed. She took off her sunglasses and turned to face Sumire. "That story reminds me of the first lecture I heard when I entered a Catholic junior high school. Did I ever tell you I went to a very strict Catholic girls' school for six years? I attended an ordinary elementary school, but I went into that school in junior high. Right after the entrance ceremony a decrepit old nun took all of us new students into the auditorium and gave a talk on Catholic ethics. She was a French nun, but her Japanese was fluent. She talked about all kinds of things, but what I recall is the story of cats and the deserted island."

"That's sounds interesting," Sumire said.

"You're shipwrecked, washed up on a deserted island. Only you and a cat made it to the lifeboat. You drift for a while and end up on this island, just a rocky island with nothing you can eat. No water, either. In your lifeboat you have ten days' worth of biscuits and water for one person, and that's it. That's how the story went.

"The nun looked all around the auditorium and she said this in a strong, clear voice. 'Close your eyes and imagine this scene. You're washed up on a deserted island with a cat. This is a solitary island in the middle of nowhere. It's almost impossible that someone would rescue you within ten days. When your food and water run out, you may very well die. Well, what would you do? Since the cat is suffering as you are, should you divide your meagre food with it?' The sister was silent again and looked at all our faces. 'No. That would be a mistake,' she continued. 'I want you to understand that dividing your food with the cat would be wrong. The reason being that you are precious beings, chosen by God, and the cat is not. That's why you should eat all the food yourself.' The nun had this terribly serious look on her face.

"At first I thought it was some kind of joke. I was waiting for the punchline. But there wasn't one. She turned her talk to the subject of human dignity and worth, and it all went over my head. I mean, really, what was the point of telling that kind of story to kids who'd just entered the school? I couldn't figure it out – and I *still* can't."

Sumire thought it over. "Do you mean whether it would be okay in the end, to eat the cat?"

"Well, I don't know. She didn't take it that far."

"Are you a Catholic?"

Miu shook her head. "That school just happened to be near my house, so I went. I liked their uniforms, too. I was the only non-Japanese citizen in the school."

"Did you have any bad experiences?"

"Because I was Korean?"

"Yes."

Again Miu shook her head. "The school was quite liberal.

The rules were pretty strict, and some of the sisters were eccentrics, but the atmosphere was generally progressive, and no, I never experienced any prejudice. I made some good friends, and overall I'd say I enjoyed school. I've had a few unpleasant experiences, but that was after I went out into the real world. But that's nothing unusual – it happens to most people."

"I heard they eat cats in Korea. Is it true?"

"I've heard the same thing. But nobody I know does."

It had been the hottest time of day, and the early afternoon town square was nearly deserted. Almost everyone in town was shut up in a cool house, taking a nap. Only curious foreigners ventured out at that time of day.

There was a statue of a hero in the square. He'd led a rebellion in mainland Greece and fought the Turks who controlled the island, but was captured and put to death by skewering. The Turks set up a sharpened stake in the square and lowered the pitiful hero onto it, naked. Ever so slowly, the stake went through his anus, and finally all the way to his mouth, taking him hours to die. The statue was supposedly erected on the spot where this happened. When it was erected, the valiant bronze statue must have been quite a sight, but over the intervening years, what with the sea wind, dust, and seagull droppings, you could barely make out the man's features. Island folk hardly gave the shabby statue a passing glance, and the statue itself looked like it had turned its back on the world.

"Speaking of cats," Sumire had blurted out, "I have a very strange memory of one. When I was in second grade we had a pretty little six-month-old tortoiseshell cat. I was on the veranda one evening, reading a book, when the cat started to run like crazy around the base of this large pine tree in the garden. Cats do that. There's nothing there, but suddenly they hiss, arch their backs, jump, hair standing on end and tail up, in attack mode.

"The cat was so worked up it didn't notice me watching it from the veranda. It was such a strange sight I laid down my book and watched the cat. It didn't seem to tire of its solitary game. Actually, as time passed it got more determined. Like it was possessed."

Sumire took a drink of water and lightly scratched her ear.

"The more I watched, the more frightened I became. The cat saw something that I couldn't see, and whatever it was drove it into a frenzy. Finally the cat started racing around and around the tree trunk at a tremendous speed, like the tiger that changes into butter in that children's story. Finally, after running forever, it leaped up the tree trunk. I could see its tiny face peeping out between the branches way up high. From the veranda I called out its name in a loud voice, but it didn't hear me.

"Finally the sun set and the cold late-autumn wind began to blow. I sat on the veranda, waiting for the cat to come down. It was a friendly cat, and I thought that if I sat there for a while, it would come down. But it didn't. I couldn't even hear it miaowing. It got darker and darker. I got scared and told my family. 'Don't worry,' they said, 'just leave it alone and it'll come down before long.' But the cat never came back."

"What do you mean – never came back?" asked Miu.

"It just disappeared. *Like smoke*. Everybody told me the

cat must have come down from the tree in the night and gone off somewhere. Cats get worked up and climb tall trees, then get frightened when they realize how high they are, and won't come down. Happens all the time. If the cat was still there, they said, it'd miaow for all it's worth to let you know. But I didn't believe that. I thought the cat must be clinging to a branch, scared to death, unable to cry out. When I came back from school, I sat on the veranda, looked at the pine tree, and every once in a while called out the cat's name. No reply. After a week, I gave up. I loved that little cat, and it made me so sad. Every time I happened to look at the pine tree I could picture that pitiful little cat, stone-cold dead, still clinging to a branch. The cat never going anywhere, starving to death and shrivelling up there."

Sumire looked at Miu.

"I never had a cat again. I still like cats, though I decided at the time that that poor little cat who climbed the tree and never returned would be my first and last cat. I couldn't forget that little cat and start loving another."

"That's what we talked about that afternoon at the café," said Miu. "I thought they were just a lot of harmless memories, but now everything seems significant. Maybe it's just my imagination."

Miu turned and looked out of the window. The breeze blowing in from the sea rustled the pleated curtains. With her gazing out at the darkness, the room seemed to acquire an even deeper silence.

"Do you mind if I ask a question? I'm sorry if it seems off the subject, but it's been bothering me," I said. "You said Sumire disappeared, vanished 'like smoke', as you put it. Four days ago. And you went to the police. Right?"

Miu nodded.

"Why did you ask me to come instead of getting in touch with Sumire's family?"

"I didn't have any clues about what happened to her. And without any solid evidence, I didn't know if I should upset her parents. I agonized over it for some time and decided to wait and see."

I tried picturing Sumire's handsome father taking the ferry to the island. Would her stepmother, understandably hurt by the turn of events, accompany him? That would be one fine mess. As far as I was concerned, though, things were already a mess. How could a foreigner possibly vanish on such a small island for four days?

"But why did you call me?"

Miu brought her bare legs together again, held the hem of her skirt between her fingers, and tugged it down.

"You were the only one I could count on."

"But you'd never met me."

"Sumire trusted you more than anyone else. She said you think deeply about things, no matter what the subject."

"Definitely a minority opinion, I'm afraid."

Miu narrowed her eyes and smiled, those tiny wrinkles appearing around her eyes.

I stood up and walked in front of her, taking her empty glass. I went into the kitchen, poured some Courvoisier into the glass, then went back to the living room. She thanked me and took the brandy. Time passed, the curtain silently fluttering. The breeze had the smell of a different place.

"Do you really, *really* want to know the truth?" Miu asked

me. She sounded drained, as if she'd come to a difficult decision.

I looked up and gazed into her face. "One thing I can say with absolute certainty," I said, "is that if I didn't want to know the truth, I wouldn't be here."

Miu squinted in the direction of the curtains. And finally spoke, in a quiet voice. "It happened that night, after we'd talked about cats at the café."

9

After their conversation at the harbour café about cats, Miu and Sumire went grocery shopping and returned to the cottage. As usual, they relaxed until dinner. Sumire was in her room, writing on her laptop. Miu lay on the sofa in the living room, hands folded behind her head, eyes closed, listening to Julius Katchen's recording of Brahms's ballads. It was an old LP, but the performance was graceful, emotional, and utterly memorable. Not a bit presumptuous, but fully expressive.

"Does the music bother you?" Miu asked once, looking in at the door to Sumire's room. The door was wide open.

"Brahms never bothers me," Sumire said, turning around.

This was the first time Miu had seen Sumire writing so intently. Her mouth was tight, like a prowling animal's, her eyes deeper than usual.

"What are you writing?" Miu asked. "A new Sputnik novel?"

The tenseness around Sumire's mouth softened a little. "Nothing much. Just things that came to mind that might be of use someday."

Miu returned to her sofa and sank back down in the miniature world the music traced in the afternoon sunlight; how wonderful it would be, she mused, to play Brahms so beautifully. In the past I always had trouble with Brahms's minor works, especially the ballads, she thought. I never could give myself up to that world of capricious, fleeting nuances and sighs. Now, though, I should be able to play Brahms more beautifully than before. But Miu knew very well: *I can't play anything. Ever again.*

At 6.30 the two of them prepared dinner in the kitchen and ate out on the veranda. A soup of sea bream and fragrant herbs, salad, and bread. They had some white wine and, later, hot coffee. They watched as a fishing boat appeared in the lee of the island and inscribed a short white arc as it sailed into the harbour. No doubt a hot meal was awaiting the fishermen in their homes.

"By the way, when will we be leaving here?" asked Sumire as she washed the dishes in the sink.

"I'd like to stay one more week, but that's about as long as I can manage," Miu replied, looking at the calendar on the wall. "If I had my way, I'd stay here for ever."

"If I had my way, me too," Sumire said, beaming. "But what can you do? Wonderful things always come to an end."

Following their usual routine, they each went to their rooms before ten. Miu changed into long-sleeve, white cotton pyjamas and fell asleep as soon as her head hit the pillow.

But soon she woke up, as if shaken by the beating of her own heart. She glanced over at the travel alarm clock next to her; it was past 12.30. The room was pitch black, enveloped by total silence. She sensed someone nearby, hiding with bated breath. Miu pulled the covers up to her neck and pricked up her ears. Her heart thumped loudly, drowning out everything else. It wasn't just a bad dream spilling over into wakefulness – someone was definitely in the room with her. Careful not to make a sound, she reached out and pulled aside the window curtain an inch or two. Pale, watery moonlight stole into the room. Keeping perfectly still, she swept the room with her eyes.

As her eyes adjusted to the dark, she could distinguish an outline of something gradually forming in a corner of the room. In the shadow of the wardrobe beside the door, where the darkness was deepest. Whatever *it* was, it was low, rolled into a thick ball like some large, long-forgotten postbag. An animal? A large dog? But the front door was locked, the door to her room shut. A dog wouldn't be able to get in.

Miu continued to breathe quietly and stared fixedly. Her mouth was dry, and she could catch a faint whiff of the brandy she'd had before going to bed. She reached out and drew the curtain back a little to let more moonlight in. Slowly, like unravelling a tangled thread, she could make out the outline of the black lump on the floor. It looked like a person's body: hair hanging down in front, two thin legs bent at an acute angle. Someone was sitting on the floor, rolled up, head between legs, scrunched up as if to protect herself from something falling from the sky.

It was Sumire. Wearing her usual blue pyjamas, she crouched like an insect between the door and the wardrobe.

Not moving. Not even breathing, as far as Miu could tell.

Miu gave a sigh of relief. But what in the world was Sumire doing here? Miu sat up quietly in bed and switched on the lamp. Yellow light lit up the entire room, but Sumire didn't budge an inch. She didn't even seem to realize the light was on.

"What's the matter?" Miu called out. First in a small voice, then more loudly.

There was no response. Miu's voice didn't appear to reach Sumire. Miu got out of bed and walked over to her. The feel of the carpet was rougher than ever against her bare feet.

"Are you sick?" Miu asked, crouching beside Sumire.

Still no answer.

Miu noticed that Sumire was holding something in her mouth. A pink facecloth that was always hanging in the bathroom. Miu tried to pull it out, but Sumire's mouth was clamped down hard. Her eyes were open, but unseeing. Miu gave up and rested a hand on her shoulder. Sumire's pyjamas were soaking wet.

"You'd better take your pyjamas off," Miu said. "You're sweating so much you'll catch cold."

Sumire looked stupefied, not hearing anything, not seeing anything. Miu decided to get Sumire's pyjamas off; otherwise her body would freeze. It was August, but sometimes nights on the island were chilly. The two of them swam nude every day and were used to seeing each other's bodies, so Miu thought Sumire wouldn't mind if she undressed her.

Supporting Sumire's body, she unbuttoned the pyjamas and, after a time, was able to get the top off. Then the bottoms. Sumire's body was rigid, but gradually relaxed and ended up limp. Miu took the facecloth out of her mouth. It was soaked from her saliva. There was a perfect set of teethmarks on it.

Sumire had no panties on under the pyjamas. Miu grabbed a towel nearby and wiped the sweat from her body. First her back, then under her arms, then her chest. She wiped her belly, then very quickly the area from her waist to her thighs. Sumire was subdued, unresisting. She appeared unconscious, though looking into her eyes Miu could make out a glint of comprehension.

Miu had never touched Sumire's naked body before. Her skin was taut, smooth like a young child's. Lifting her up, Miu found that Sumire's body was heavier than she had imagined, and smelled of sweat. Wiping the sweat from her, Miu felt again her own heart thumping in her chest. Saliva gathered in her mouth, and she had to swallow again and again.

Bathed in moonlight, Sumire's body glistened like some ancient ceramic. Her breasts were small, but shapely, with well-formed nipples. Her black pubic hair was wet with sweat and glittered like grass in the morning dew. Her limp, naked body was completely different from the one Miu had seen under the blazing sun at the beach. Her body was a mix of still-girlish elements and a budding maturity blindly wrenched open by the painful flow of time.

Miu felt like she was peering into someone's else's secrets, something forbidden she shouldn't be seeing. She avoided looking at her naked skin as she continued to wipe away the sweat from Sumire's body, all the while replaying in her mind a Bach piece she'd memorized as a child. She wiped Sumire's sweaty fringe, which was plastered to her forehead. Even the inside of Sumire's tiny ears were sweaty.

Miu felt Sumire's arm silently go around her own body. Sumire's breath grazed her neck.

"All you all right?" she asked.

Sumire didn't reply. But her arm held on a bit more tightly. Half carrying her, Miu helped her into her own bed. She lay her down and pulled the covers over her. Sumire lay there, unmoving, and closed her eyes.

Miu watched her for a while, but Sumire didn't move a muscle. She seemed to have fallen asleep. Miu went to the kitchen and gulped down several glasses of mineral water. She took a few deep breaths and managed to calm down. Her heart had stopped pounding, though her chest ached with the tension of the last few moments. Everything was cloaked in a choking silence. No voices, not even a dog barking. No waves, no sound of the wind. Why, Miu wondered, is everything so deadly still?

Miu went into the bathroom and took Sumire's sweaty pyjamas, the towel she'd used to wipe her down, and the facecloth with the teethmarks and tossed them into the laundry basket. She washed her face and gazed at her reflection in the mirror. Since coming to the island she hadn't dyed her hair, which was now pure white, like newly fallen snow.

When Miu went back into the room Sumire's eyes were open. A thin, translucent veil seemed to cover them, but a glimmer of consciousness had returned. She lay there, the covers up to her shoulders.

"I'm sorry," she said huskily. "Sometimes I get this way."

Miu sat down on a corner of the bed, smiled, and reached out to touch Sumire's still-damp hair. "You should take a good, long shower. You were really sweating."

"Thanks," said Sumire. "I just want to lie here."

Miu nodded and handed Sumire a fresh bath towel, took out a pair of her own clean pyjamas from the chest of drawers and laid them beside Sumire. "You can use these. I don't imagine you have another pair, do you?"

"Can I sleep here tonight?" asked Sumire.

"All right. Just go to sleep. I'll sleep in your bed."

"My bed must be soaked," Sumire said. "The covers, everything. And I don't want to be alone. Don't leave me here. Would you sleep beside me? Just for tonight? I don't want to have any more nightmares."

Miu thought about it, then nodded. "But first put on a pair of pyjamas. I don't think I'd like having somebody naked lying right next to me – especially in such a small bed."

Sumire got up slowly and pushed back the covers. She stood up, still naked, and tugged on Miu's pyjamas. She leaned forward and slipped on the bottoms, then the top. It took some time to get the buttons all fastened. Her fingers wouldn't work right. Miu didn't help, she just sat there watching. Sumire buttoned up the pyjamas in such a deliberate way it struck Miu as an almost religious ceremony. The moonlight lent a strange hardness to her nipples.

She might be a virgin, Miu suddenly thought.

After putting on the silk pyjamas, Sumire lay down again in bed, on the far side. Miu got into bed, where the scent of sweat remained strong.

"Can I," Sumire began, "just hold you for a while?"

"Hold me?"

"Yes."

While Miu wondered how to respond, Sumire reached

out and clasped her hand. Her palm was still sweaty, warm and soft. She reached both hands behind Miu. Sumire's breasts pushed against Miu, just above her stomach. Sumire pressed her cheek between Miu's breasts. They remained that way for a long time. Sumire seemed to be shaking, ever so slightly. She must be crying, Miu thought. But it was as if she couldn't let it all out. Miu reached around Sumire's shoulder and drew her closer. She's still a child, Miu thought. Lonely and frightened, she wants someone's warmth. Like that kitten clinging to a pine branch.

Sumire shifted her body upwards a bit. The tip of her nose brushed Miu's neck. Their breasts pressed together. Miu gulped. Sumire's hand wandered over her back.

"I really like you," Sumire said in a small voice.

"I like you, too," Miu said. She didn't know what else to say. And it was the truth.

Sumire's fingers started to unbutton the front of Miu's pyjamas. Miu tried to stop her. But Sumire wouldn't stop. "Just a little," she said. "Just a little – *please*."

Miu lay there unresisting. Sumire's fingers gently traced the contours of Miu's breasts. Her nose flickered back and forth at Miu's throat. She touched Miu's nipple, stroked it gently, and held it between two fingers. Hesitantly at first, then more boldly.

Miu stopped speaking. She looked up, searchingly, at me. Her cheeks were slightly flushed.

"There's something I need to explain to you. A long time ago I had a very unusual experience, and my hair turned pure white. Overnight, completely. Since then I've dyed my hair. Sumire knew I dyed it, and since it was too much trouble after we came to this island, I gave up. Nobody knows me here, so it didn't matter. But knowing you'd be coming, I dyed it again. I didn't want to give you a strange first impression."

Time flowed past in the ensuing silence.

"I've never had a homosexual experience, and never considered I had those tendencies. But if that's what Sumire really wanted, I thought I could oblige. At least I didn't find it disgusting. As long as it was with *Sumire*, that is. So I didn't resist when she started feeling me all over, or when she stuck her tongue inside my mouth. It felt strange, but I tried to get used to it. I let her do what she wanted. I like Sumire, and if it made her happy, I didn't mind what she did.

"But my body and my mind are two different things. A part of me was happy that Sumire was caressing me so lovingly. But no matter how happy my mind was, my body resisted. It wouldn't yield to her. My heart and my head were aroused, but the rest of me was like a hard, dry stone. It's sad, but I couldn't help it. Of course Sumire picked up on that. Her body was flushed and gently damp, but I couldn't respond.

"I told her how I felt. 'I'm not rejecting you,' I said, 'but I just can't do that kind of thing. Ever since *that* happened to me, 14 years ago, I haven't been able to give myself to anyone in *this* world. It's something that's out of my hands, decided somewhere else.' I told her that if there was anything I could do, you know, with my fingers, or mouth, I would. But that isn't what she wanted. I knew that already."

"She kissed me on the forehead and said she was sorry. 'It's just that I like you,' she said. 'I've worried about it for so long, and I had to try.' 'I like you, too,' I told her. 'So don't worry about it. I still want you to be with me.'

"As if a dam had burst, Sumire sobbed into her pillow for the longest time. As she cried, I rubbed her bare back from the top of her shoulder to her waist, feeling all her bones. I wanted to cry along with her, but I couldn't.

"And it came to me then. That we were wonderful travelling companions, but in the end no more than lonely lumps of metal on their own separate orbits. From far off they look like beautiful shooting stars, but in reality they're nothing more than prisons, where each of us is locked up alone, going nowhere. When the orbits of these two satellites of ours happened to cross paths, we could be together. Maybe even open our hearts to each other. But that was only for the briefest moment. In the next instant we'd be in absolute solitude. Until we burned up and became nothing."

"After crying her heart out, Sumire got up, picked up the pyjamas that had fallen to the floor and slipped them on," said Miu. "She said she wanted to be alone and was going back to her room. 'Don't think too deeply about things,' I told her. 'Tomorrow's a new day, things will work out just like before. You'll see.' 'I guess so,' Sumire said. She leaned over and held her cheek against mine. Her cheek was wet and warm. She whispered something in my ear, I think. But in such a small voice I couldn't make it out. I was about to ask her what she said, but she'd already turned away."

*

"Sumire wiped her tears away with the bath towel and left the room. The door closed, and I snuggled back under the covers and closed my eyes. After an experience like that, I thought it would be hard to sleep, but strangely enough I soon fell fast asleep.

"When I woke up at seven the next morning, Sumire was nowhere in the house. Perhaps she woke up early – or maybe never got back to sleep – and went to the beach by herself. She said she wanted to be alone for a while. It was odd that she didn't even leave a note, but considering the night before, I guessed she was still pretty upset and confused.

"I did the washing, hung out her bedding to dry, and sat on the veranda, reading, waiting for her to come back. The whole morning passed, and no Sumire. I was worried, so I looked through her room, even though I knew I shouldn't. I was afraid maybe she'd left the island. But her bags were still open, her passport was still in her handbag, her swimsuit and socks drying in a corner of her room. Coins, notepaper, and a bunch of keys lay scattered on her desk. One of the keys was for the front door of the cottage.

"It all felt weird to me. What I mean is whenever we went to the beach we always wore heavy trainers and T-shirts over our swimsuits as we walked over the mountains. With a canvas bag with our towels and mineral water. But she'd left it all behind – the bag, shoes, and swimsuit. The only things missing were the pair of cheap flip-flops she'd bought at a local shop and the pair of thin silk pyjamas I'd lent her. Even if you only meant to take a walk around the neighbourhood, you wouldn't stay out long dressed like that, would you?

"In the afternoon I went out to scour the area for her. I made a couple of circuits nearby, went to the beach, then walked back and forth down the streets of the town, and finally returned home. But Sumire was nowhere to be found. The sun was setting, and night came on. The wind had picked up. All night long I could hear the sound of the waves. Any little sound woke me up. I left the front door unlocked. Dawn came, and still no Sumire. Her bed was just as I'd left it. So I went down to the local police station near the harbour."

"I explained everything to one of the policemen, one who spoke English. 'The girl who was travelling with me has disappeared,' I told him, 'and hasn't been back for two nights.' He didn't take me seriously. 'Your friend will be back,' he said. It happens all the time. Everyone lets their hair down here. It's summer, they're young, what do you expect?' I went again the next day, and this time they paid a bit more attention. Not that they were going to do anything about it. I phoned the Japanese embassy in Athens and explained the situation. Thankfully, the person there was quite kind. He said something in no uncertain terms in Greek to the police chief, and the police finally started getting an investigation up and running.

"They were simply clueless. They questioned people in the harbour and around our cottage, but no one had seen Sumire. The captain of the ferry, and the man who sold ferry tickets, had no recollection of any young Japanese girl getting on the boat in the last couple of days. Sumire must still be on the island. She didn't have any money on her to buy a ticket in the first place. On this little island a young Japanese girl wandering about in pyjamas wouldn't escape people's notice. The police questioned a German couple who'd been swimming for a long time that morning at the beach. They hadn't seen any Japanese girl, either at the beach or on the road there. The police promised me they'd continue to do their best, and I think they did. But time passed without a single clue."

Miu took a deep breath and covered half her face with her hands.

"All I could do was call you in Tokyo and ask you to come. I was at my wits' end."

I pictured Sumire, alone, wandering the rugged hills in a pair of thin silk pyjamas and flip-flops.

"What colour were the pyjamas?" I asked.

"Colour?" said Miu, a dubious look on her face.

"The pyjamas Sumire was wearing when she disappeared."

"What colour were they? I'm not sure. I bought them in Milan and hadn't worn them yet. A light colour. Pale green, maybe? They were very lightweight, with no pockets."

"I'd like you to call the embassy in Athens again and ask them to send somebody here. Insist on it. Then have the embassy contact Sumire's parents. It'll be hard on them, but you can't keep it from them any more."

Miu gave a small nod.

"Sumire can be a little outrageous at times, as you know," I said, "and she does the craziest things. But she wouldn't leave for four days without a word. She's not that irresponsible. She wouldn't disappear unless there's a very good reason. What reason, I don't know, but it must be serious. Maybe she fell down a well out in the country, and she's waiting for someone to rescue her. Maybe somebody kidnapped her. For all we know she could be murdered and buried somewhere. A young girl wandering at night in pyjamas – anything could happen. At any rate, we've got to come up with a plan. But let's sleep on it. Tomorrow's going to be a long day."

"Do you think maybe . . . Sumire . . . killed herself?" Miu asked.

"We can't rule that out. But she would have left a note. She wouldn't have left everything scattered like this for you to pick up the pieces. She liked you, and I know she would consider your feelings."

Arms folded, Miu looked at me for a while. "You *really* think so?"

I nodded. "Absolutely. That's the way she is."

"Thank you. That's what I wanted to hear most."

Miu led me to Sumire's room. Devoid of decorations, the boxy room reminded me of a big cube. There was a small wooden bed, a writing desk, a wardrobe, and a small dresser. At the foot of the desk was an average-size red suitcase. The front window was open to the hills beyond. On top of the desk was a brand new Macintosh PowerBook.

"I've straightened up her things so you can sleep here."

Left alone, I grew suddenly sleepy. It was nearly midnight. I undressed and got under the covers, but I couldn't sleep. Until just a while ago, I thought, Sumire was sleeping in this bed. The excitement of the long trip reverberated in my body. I was struck by the illusion that I was on a journey without end.

In bed I reviewed everything Miu had told me, making a mental list of the important points. But my mind wouldn't work. Systematic thought was beyond me. Leave it for tomorrow, I concluded. Out of the blue, the image came to me of Sumire's tongue inside Miu's mouth. Forget about it, I willed my brain. Leave that for tomorrow as well. But the chances of tomorrow being an improvement on today were, unfortunately, slim. Gloomy thoughts weren't going to get me anywhere, I decided, and closed my eyes. I soon fell into a deep sleep.

10

When I woke up, Miu was setting the table for breakfast out on the veranda. It was 8.30, and a brand-new sun was flooding the world with sunlight. Miu and I sat down on the veranda and had breakfast, gazing at the bright sea as we ate. We had toast and eggs and coffee. Two white birds glided down the slope towards the coast. A radio was playing nearby, an announcer's voice, speaking quickly, reading the news in Greek.

A strange jet-lag numbness filled my head. I couldn't separate the boundary between what was real and what only seemed real. Here I was on a small Greek island, sharing a meal with a beautiful older woman I'd met only the day before. This woman loved Sumire, but couldn't feel any sexual desire for her. Sumire loved this woman and desired her. I loved Sumire and felt sexual desire for her. Sumire liked me, but didn't love me, and didn't feel any desire for me. I felt sexual desire for a woman who will remain anonymous. But I didn't love her. It was all so complicated, like something out of an existential play. Everything hit a dead end there, no alternatives left. And Sumire had exited stage right.

Miu refilled my empty coffee cup. I thanked her.

"You like Sumire, don't you?" Miu asked me. "As a woman, I mean."

I gave a slight nod as I buttered my toast. The butter was cold and hard, and it took some time to spread it on the bread. I looked up and added, "Of course that's not something you necessarily can choose. It just happens."

We continued eating breakfast in silence. The news ended, and the radio started to play Greek music. The wind swelled up and shook the bougainvilleas. If you looked closely, you could make out whitecaps appearing.

"I've given it a great deal of thought, and I think I should go to Athens right away," Miu said, peeling some fruit. "I'd probably get nowhere over the phone, so it'd be better if I went straight to the embassy and talked with them face to face. Maybe someone from the embassy will be willing to come back with me, or I might wait for Sumire's parents to arrive in Athens and come back with them. At any rate, I'd like you to stay here as long as you can. The police might get in touch, and there's always the possibility that Sumire will come back. Would you do that for me?"

Of course, I replied.

"I'm going to go to the police station again to check on the investigation, then charter a boat to take me to Rhodes. A return trip to Athens takes time, so most likely I'll get a hotel room and stay a couple of days."

I nodded.

Miu finished peeling the orange and wiped it carefully with a napkin. "Have you ever met Sumire's parents?"

I never have, I said.

Miu gave a sigh like the wind at the edge of the world. "I wonder how I'm going to explain it to them."

I could understand her confusion. How can you explain the inexplicable?

Miu and I walked down to the harbour. She had a small bag with a change of clothes, wore leather high-heeled shoes, and carried a Mila Schön shoulder bag. We stopped by the police station. We told them I was a relative of Miu's who happened to be travelling nearby. They still didn't have a single clue. "But it's all right," they said cheerily. "Not to worry. Look around you. This is a peaceful island. We have some crime, of course – lovers' quarrels, drunks, political fights. We're dealing with people, after all, and everywhere you go it's the same. But those are domestic squabbles. In the last 15 years there's never once been a foreigner who's been the victim of a crime on this island."

That might very well be true. But when it came to explaining Sumire's disappearance, they had nothing to say.

"There's a large limestone cave on the north shore of the island," the police ventured. "If she wandered in there, maybe she couldn't find her way out. It's like a maze inside. But it's very, very far away. A girl like that couldn't have walked that far."

Could she have drowned? I asked.

The policemen shook their heads. There's no strong

current around here, they said. And the weather this past week has been mild, the sea calm. Lots of fishermen go out to fish every day, and if the girl had drowned, one of them would have come across her body.

"What about wells?" I asked. "Couldn't she have fallen in a deep well somewhere while she was out for a walk?"

The chief of police shook his head. "There aren't any wells on the island. We have a lot of natural springs so there's no need to dig any. Besides, the bedrock is hard and digging a well would be a major undertaking."

After we left the police station I told Miu I wanted to walk to the beach she and Sumire had frequented, if possible in the morning. She bought a simple map of the island at a kiosk and showed me the road; it takes 45 minutes one way, she cautioned, so be sure to wear some sturdy shoes. She went to the harbour and, in a mixture of French and English, quickly concluded negotiations with the pilot of a small taxi boat to take her to Rhodes.

"If only we had a happy ending," Miu said as she left. But her eyes told another story. She knew that things didn't work out that simply. And so did I. The boat's engine started up, and she held down her hat with her left hand and waved to me with her right. When her boat disappeared offshore, I felt like my insides were missing a couple of parts. I wandered around the harbour for a while and bought some dark sunglasses at a souvenir shop. Then I climbed the steep stairs back to the cottage.

As the sun rose higher it grew fiercely hot. I put a short-sleeve cotton shirt on over my trunks, put on my sunglasses

138

and jogging shoes, and set off over the steep mountain road to the beach. I soon regretted not bringing a hat, but decided to forge on. I soon got thirsty walking uphill. I stopped and took a drink and rubbed the sunscreen Miu had lent me over my face and arms. The path was white with dust, which swirled into the air whenever the wind blew. Occasionally I'd pass villagers leading donkeys. They'd greet me in a loud voice: *"Kali mera!"* I'd say the same thing back to them. I supposed it was the thing to do.

The mountainside was covered with short, twisted trees. Mountain goats and sheep made their way over the craggy rock face, crabby looks on their faces. The bells around their necks made a matter-of-fact little tinkling sound. The people herding the flocks were either children or old people. As I passed they'd glance at me out of the corner of their eyes and then half raise their hand in some sort of sign. I raised my hand the same way in greeting. Sumire couldn't have come this way by herself. There was no place to hide, and someone would have seen her.

The beach was deserted. I took off my shirt and trunks and swam in the nude. The water was clear and felt wonderful. You could see all the way to the stones on the bottom. A yacht was anchored at the mouth of the inlet, sail stowed, and the tall mast swayed back and forth like a giant metronome. Nobody was on deck. Each time the tide went out, countless little stones were left behind, clattering listlessly. After swimming, I went back to the beach and lay down, still naked, on my towel and gazed up at the high, pure blue sky. Seabirds circled above the inlet searching for fish. The sky was utterly cloudless. I dozed there for perhaps half an hour, during which time no one visited the beach. Before long a strange hush fell over me. This beach was a little too quiet for a person to visit alone, a little *too* beautiful. It made me imagine a certain way of dying. I dressed and walked over the mountain path, back towards the cottage. The heat was even more intense than before. Mechanically moving one foot after the other, I tried to imagine what Sumire and Miu must have talked about when the two of them walked this road together.

Sumire might very well have been pondering the sexual desire she felt. The same way I thought about my own desire when I was with her. It wasn't hard for me to understand how she felt. Sumire pictured Miu naked beside her and wanted nothing so much as to hold her tight. An expectation was there, mixed with so many other emotions – excitement, resignation, hesitation, confusion, fear – that would well up, then wither on the vine. You're optimistic one moment, only to be wracked the next by the surety that it will all fall to pieces. And in the end it does.

I walked to the top of the mountain, took a break and a drink of water, then headed downhill. Just as the roof of the cottage came into view, I remembered what Miu had said about Sumire feverishly writing something in her room after they came to the island. What could she have been writing? Miu hadn't said anything more, and I didn't push it. There might – just *might* – be a clue in what Sumire wrote. I could have kicked myself for not having thought of it before.

When I got back to the cottage I went to Sumire's room, turned on her PowerBook, and opened the hard drive. Nothing looked promising. There was a list of expenses for their European trip, addresses, a schedule. All business items related to Miu's work. No personal files. I opened the RECENT DOCUMENTS menu – nothing. She probably didn't want anybody to read it and had erased it all. Which meant that she had saved her personal files on a floppy disk somewhere. It was unlikely she'd taken the disk with her when she disappeared; for one thing, her pyjamas didn't have any pockets.

I rummaged around in the desk drawers. There were a couple of disks, but they were copies of what was on the hard drive or other work-related files. Nothing looked promising. I sat at the desk and thought. If I were Sumire, where would I put it? The room was small; there weren't many places to hide something. Sumire was very particular about deciding who could read what she wrote.

Of course – the red suitcase. This was the only thing in the room that could be locked.

Her new suitcase seemed empty, it was so light; I shook it, but it didn't make any sound. The four-digit padlock was locked, however. I tried several combinations of numbers I knew Sumire was likely to use – her birthday, her address, telephone number, post code – but none of them worked. Not surprising, since a number that someone could easily guess wasn't much use as a combination number. It had to be something she could remember, but that wasn't based on something personal. I thought about it for a long time, and then it hit me. I tried the area code for Kunitachi – *my* area code, in other words. 0-4-2-5.

The lock clicked open.

A small black cloth bag was stuck inside the inner side pocket of the suitcase. I unzipped it and found a little green

141

diary and a floppy disk inside. I opened the diary first. It was written in her usual handwriting. Nothing leaped out at me. It was just information about where they went. Who they saw. Names of hotels. The price of petrol. Dinner menus. Brands of wine and what they tasted like. Basically just a list. A lot of the pages were blank. Keeping a diary wasn't one of Sumire's strong points, apparently.

The disk was untitled. The label just had the date on it, in Sumire's distinctive handwriting. August 19**. I slipped the disk inside the PowerBook and opened it. The menu showed two documents, neither of which had a title. They were just Document 1 and Document 2.

Before opening them, I slowly looked around the room. Sumire's coat was hanging in the wardrobe. I saw her goggles, her Italian dictionary, her passport. Inside the desk were her ballpoint pen and propelling pencil. In the window above the desk the gentle, craggy slope was visible. A black cat was walking on top of the wall of the house next door. The bare little box room was enveloped in the late afternoon silence. I closed my eyes and could still hear the waves on the deserted beach that morning. I opened my eyes again, and this time listened closely to the real world. I couldn't hear a thing.

I set my pointer on Document 1 and double-clicked the icon.

11

Document 1

Did You Ever See Anyone Shot by a Gun without Bleeding?

Fate has led me to a conclusion – an ad hoc conclusion, mind you (is there any other kind? interesting question, but I'll leave it for some other time) – and here I am on an island in Greece. A small island whose name I'd never even heard of until recently. The time is . . . a little past four in the morning. Still dark out, of course. Innocent goats have slipped into their peaceful, collective sleep. The line of olive trees outside in the field is sipping at the nourishment the darkness provides. And the moon, like some melancholy priest, rests above the rooftop, stretching out its hands to the barren sea.

No matter where I find myself, this is the time of day I love best. The time that's mine alone. It'll be dawn soon, and I'm sitting here writing. Like Buddha, born from his mother's side (the right or the left, I can't recall), the new sun will lumber up and peek over the edge of the hills. And the ever discreet Miu will quietly wake up. At six we'll make a simple breakfast together, and afterwards go over the hills to our ever lovely beach. Before this routine begins, I want to roll up my sleeves and finish a bit of work.

Except for a few letters, it's been a long time since I've written something purely for myself, and I'm not very confident I can express myself the way I'd like to. Not that I've ever had that confidence. Somehow, though, I always feel *driven* to write.

Why? It's simple, really. In order for me to think about something, I have to first put it into writing.

It's been that way since I was little. When I didn't understand something, I gathered up the words scattered at my feet, and lined them up into sentences. If that didn't help, I'd scatter them again, rearrange them in a different order. Repeat that a number of times, and I was able to think about things like most people. Writing for me was never difficult. Other children gathered pretty stones or acorns, and I *wrote*. As naturally as breathing, I'd scribble down one sentence after another. And I'd *think*.

No doubt you think it's a time-consuming process to reach a conclusion, seeing as how every time I thought about something I had to go through all those steps. Or maybe you wouldn't think that. But in *actual practice* it did take time. So much so that by the time I entered elementary school people thought I was retarded. I couldn't keep up with the other kids.

When I finished elementary school the feeling of alienation this gave me had lessened considerably. By then I'd found a way to keep pace with the world around me. Still, until I left college and broke off any relations with officialdom, this gap existed inside me – like a silent snake in the grass.

My provisional theme here: On a day-to-day basis I use writing to work out who I am.

*

144

Right?
Right you are!

I've written an incredible amount up till now. Nearly every day. It's like I was standing in a huge pasture, cutting the grass all by myself, and the grass grows back almost as fast as I can cut it. Today I'd cut over here, tomorrow over there . . . By the time I make one complete round of the pasture the grass in the first spot is as tall as it was in the beginning.

But since I met Miu I've barely written. Why is that? The Fiction = Transmission theory K. told me does make sense. On one level there's some truth to it. But it doesn't explain everything. I've got to simplify my thinking here.

Simplify, simplify.

What happened after I met Miu was I stopped *thinking*. (Of course I'm using my own individual definition of *thinking* here.) Miu and I were always together, two interlocking spoons, and with her I was swept away somewhere – someplace I couldn't fathom – and I just thought, Okay, go with the flow.

In other words, I had to get rid of a lot of baggage to get closer to her. Even the act of thinking became a burden. I think that explains it. No matter how tall the grass got, I couldn't be bothered. I sprawled on my back, gazing up at the sky, watching the billowy clouds drift by. Consigning my fate to the clouds. Giving myself up to the pungent aroma of the grass, the murmur of the wind. And after a time I couldn't have cared less about the difference between what I knew and what I didn't know.

No, that's not true. *From day one* I couldn't have cared less. I have to be a bit more precise in my account here.

Precision, precision.

*

I see now that my basic rule of thumb in writing has always been to write about things as if I *didn't* know them – and this would include things that I did know, or thought I knew about. If I said from the beginning, *Oh, I know that, no need to spend my precious time writing about it,* my writing would never have got off the ground. For example, if I think about somebody, *I know that guy, no need to spend time thinking about him, I've got him down,* I run the risk of being betrayed (and this would apply to you as well). On the flip side of everything we think we absolutely understand lurks an equal amount of the *unknown*.

Understanding is but the sum of our misunderstandings.

Just between us, that's my way of comprehending the world. In a nutshell.

In the world we live in, what we *know* and what we *don't know* are like Siamese twins, inseparable, existing in a state of confusion.

Confusion, confusion.

Who can really distinguish between the sea and what's reflected in it? Or tell the difference between the falling rain and loneliness?

Without any fuss, then, I gave up worrying about the difference between knowing and *not* knowing. That became my point of departure. A terrible place to start, perhaps – but people need a makeshift springboard, right? All of which goes to explain how I started seeing dualisms such as theme and style, object and subject, cause and effect, the joints of my hand and the rest of me, not as black-and-white pairs, but as indistinguishable one from the other. Everything had spilled on the kitchen floor – the salt, pepper, flour, starch. All mixed into one fine blob.

*

The joints of my hand and the rest of me . . . I notice sitting here in front of the computer that I'm back to my old bad habit of cracking my knuckles. This bad habit made quite a comeback after I stopped smoking. First I crack the joints of the five fingers of my right hand – *crack crack* – then the joints of my left hand. I'm not trying to brag, but I can crack my joints so loud you'd think someone's neck's getting broken. I was the champion knuckle-cracker in elementary school. Put the boys to shame.

When I was at college, K. let me know in no uncertain terms that this wasn't exactly a skill I should be proud of. When a girl reaches a certain age she can't be snapping her knuckles all over the place. Especially in front of other people. Otherwise you'll end up like Lotte Lenya in *From Russia with Love*. Now why hadn't anybody ever told me that before? I tried to break the habit. I mean, I really like Lotte Lenya, but not enough to want to *be* her. Once I stopped smoking, though, I realized that whenever I sat down to write, unconsciously I was cracking my knuckles all over again. *Snap crackle pop*.

The name's Bond. James Bond.

Let me get back to what I was saying. Time's limited – no room for detours. Forget Lotte Lenya. Sorry, metaphors – gotta split. As I said before, inside us what we know and what we don't know share the same abode. For convenience's sake most people erect a wall between them. It makes life easier. But I just swept that wall away. I *had* to. I hate walls. That's just the kind of person I am.

To use the image of the Siamese twins again, it's not like they always get along. They don't always try to understand each other. In fact the opposite is more often true. The right hand doesn't try to know what the left hand's doing – and vice versa. Confusion reigns, we end up lost – and we crash smack-bang right into something. *Thud*.

What I'm getting at is that people have to come up with a clever strategy if they want what they know and what they don't know to live together in peace. And that strategy – yep, you've got it! – is *thinking*. We have to find a secure anchor. Otherwise, no mistake about it, we're on an awful *collision course*.

A question.

So what are people supposed to do if they want to avoid a collision (*thud!*) but still lie in the field, enjoying the clouds drifting by, listening to the grass grow – not thinking, in other words? Sounds hard? Not at all. Logically, it's easy. *C'est simple*. The answer is *dreams*. Dreaming on and on. Entering the world of dreams, and never coming out. Living in dreams for the rest of time.

In dreams you don't need to make any distinctions between things. Not at all. Boundaries don't exist. So in dreams there are hardly ever collisions. Even if there are, they don't hurt. Reality is different. Reality bites.

Reality, reality.

Way back when the Sam Peckinpah film *The Wild Bunch* premiered, a woman journalist raised her hand at the press conference and asked the following: "Why in the world do you have to show so much blood all over the place?" She was pretty worked up about it. One of the actors, Ernest Borgnine, looked a bit perplexed and fielded the question. "Lady, did you ever see anyone shot by a gun without bleeding?" This film came out at the height of the Vietnam War.

I love that line. That's gotta be one of the principles behind reality. Accepting things that are hard to comprehend, and leaving them that way. And bleeding. Shooting and bleeding.

Did you ever see anyone shot by a gun without bleeding?

Which explains my stance as a writer. I think – in a very ordinary way – and reach a point where, in a realm I cannot even give a name to, I conceive a dream, a sightless foetus called *understanding*, floating in the universal, overwhelming amniotic fluid of incomprehension. Which must be why my novels are absurdly long and, up till now, at least, never reach a proper conclusion. The technical, and moral, skills needed to maintain a supply line on that scale are beyond me.

Of course I'm not writing a novel here. I don't know what to call it. Just writing. I'm thinking aloud, so there's no need to wrap things up neatly. I have no moral obligations. I'm merely – hmm – *thinking*. I haven't done any real thinking for the longest time, and probably won't for the foreseeable future. But right now, at this very moment, I *am* thinking. And that's what I'm going to do until morning. Think.

That being said, though, I can't rid myself of my old familiar dark doubts. Aren't I spending all my time and energy in some useless pursuit? Hauling a bucket of water to a place that's on the verge of flooding? Shouldn't I give up any useless effort and just go with the flow?

Collision? What's that?

149

Let me put it a different way.

Okay – what different way was I going to use?

Oh, I remember – this is what it is.

If I'm going to merely ramble, maybe I should just snuggle under the warm covers, think of Miu, and play with myself. That's what I meant.

I love the curve of Miu's rear end. The exquisite contrast between her jet-black pubic hair and snow-white hair, the nicely shaped arse, clad in tiny black panties. Talk about sexy. Inside her black panties, her T-shaped pubic hair, every bit as black.

I've got to stop thinking about that. Switch off the circuit of pointless sexual fantasies (*click*) and concentrate on writing. Can't let these precious pre-dawn moments slip away. I'll let somebody else, in some other context, decide what's effective and what isn't. Right now I don't have a glass of barley tea's worth of interest in what they might say.

Right?
Right you are!
So – onward and upward.

They say it's a dangerous experiment to include dreams (actual dreams or otherwise) in the fiction you write. Only a handful of writers – and I'm talking the most talented – are able to pull off the kind of irrational synthesis you find in dreams. Sounds reasonable. Still, I want to relate a dream, one I had recently. I want to record this dream simply as a fact that concerns me and my life. Whether it's literary or not, I don't care. I'm just the keeper of the warehouse.

*

I've had the same type of dream many times. The details differ, including the setting, but they all follow the same pattern. And the pain I feel upon waking is always the same. A single theme is repeated there over and over, like a train blowing its whistle at the same blind curve night after night.

Sumire's Dream

(I've written this in the third person. It feels more authentic that way.)

Sumire is climbing a long spiral staircase to meet her mother, who died a long time ago. Her mother is waiting at the top of the stairs. She has something she wants to tell Sumire, a critical piece of information Sumire desperately needs in order to live. Sumire's never met a dead person before, and she's afraid. She doesn't know what kind of person her mother is. Maybe – for some reason Sumire can't imagine – her mother hates her. But she has to meet her. This is her one and only chance.

The stairs go on forever. Climb and climb and she still doesn't reach the top. Sumire rushes up the stairs, out of breath. She's running out of time. Her mother won't always be here, in this building. Sumire's brow breaks out in a sweat. And finally the stairs come to an end.

At the top of the staircase there's a broad landing, a thick stone wall at the very end facing her. Right at eye level there's a kind of round hole like a ventilation shaft. A small hole about 20 inches in diameter. And Sumire's mother, as if she'd been pushed inside feet first, is crammed inside that hole. Sumire realizes that her time is nearly up.

In that cramped space, her mother faces outwards, towards her. She looks at Sumire's face as if appealing to her. Sumire knows in a glance that it's her mother. She's the person who gave me life and flesh, she realizes. But somehow the woman here is not the mother in the family photo album. My real mother is beautiful, and youthful. So that person in the album wasn't really my mother after all, Sumire thinks. My father tricked me.

"Mother!" Sumire bravely shouts. She feels a wall of sorts melt away inside her. No sooner does she utter this word than her mother is pulled deeper into that hole, as if sucked by some giant vacuum on the other side. Her mother's mouth is open, and she's shouting something to Sumire. But the hollow sound of the wind rushing out of the hole swallows up her words. In the next instant her mother is yanked into the darkness of the hole and vanishes.

Sumire looks back, and the staircase is gone. She's surrounded by stone walls. Where the staircase had been there's a wooden door. She turns the knob and opens the door, and beyond is the sky. She's at the top of a tall tower. So high it makes her dizzy to look down. Lots of tiny objects, like aeroplanes, are buzzing around in the sky. Simple little planes anybody could make, constructed of bamboo and light pieces of lumber. In the rear of each plane there's a tiny fist-sized engine and propeller. Sumire yells out to one of the passing pilots to come and rescue her. But none of the pilots pays any attention.

It must be because I'm wearing these clothes, Sumire decides. Nobody can see me. She has on an anonymous white hospital gown. She takes it off, and is naked – there's nothing on underneath. She discards the gown on the ground next to the door, and like a soul now unfettered it catches an updraught and sails out of sight. The same wind caresses her body, rustles the hair between her legs. With a start she notices that all the little aeroplanes have changed into dragonflies. The sky is filled with multicoloured dragonflies, their huge bulbous eyes glistening as they gaze around. The buzz of their wings grows steadily louder, like a radio being turned up. Finally it's an unbearable roar. Sumire crouches down, eyes closed, and covers her ears.

And she wakes up.

Sumire could recall every last detail of the dream. She could have painted a picture of it. The only thing she couldn't recall was her mother's face as it was sucked into that black hole. And the critical words her mother spoke, too, were lost for ever in that vacant void. In bed, Sumire violently bit her pillow and cried and cried.

The Barber Won't Be Digging Any More Holes

After this dream I came to an important decision. The tip of my somewhat industrious pickaxe will finally begin to chip away at the solid cliff. *Thwack.* I decided to make it clear to Miu what I want. I can't stay like this forever, hanging. I can't be like a spineless little barber digging a hole in his back garden, revealing to no one the fact that I love Miu. Act that way and slowly but surely I will fade away. All the dawns and all the twilights will rob me, piece by piece, of myself, and before long my very life will be shaved away completely – and I would end up *nothing*.

*

153

Matters are as clear as crystal.

Crystal, crystal.

I want to make love to Miu, and be held by her. I've already surrendered so much that's important to me. There's nothing more I can give up. It's not too late. I have to *be* with Miu, enter her. And she must enter me. Like two greedy, glistening snakes.

And if Miu doesn't accept me, then what?

I'll cross that bridge when the times comes.

"Did you ever see anyone shot by a gun without bleeding?"

Blood must be shed. I'll sharpen my knife, ready to slit a dog's throat somewhere.

Right?

Right you are!

What I've written here is a message to myself. I toss it into the air like a boomerang. It slices through the dark, lays the little soul of some poor kangaroo out cold, and finally comes back to me.

But the boomerang that returns is not the same one I threw.

Boomerang, boomerang.

12

Document 2

It's 2.30 in the afternoon. Outside it's as bright and hot as hell. The cliffs, the sky, and the sea are sparkling. Look at them long enough and the boundaries begin to dissolve, everything melting into a chaotic ooze. Consciousness sinks into the sleepy shadows to avoid the light. Even the birds have given up flying. Inside the house, though, it's pleasantly cool. Miu is in the living room listening to Brahms. She's wearing a blue summer dress with thin straps, her pure-white hair pulled back simply. I'm at my desk, writing these words.

"Does the music bother you?" Miu asks me.

Brahms never bothers me, I answer.

I've been searching my memory, trying to reproduce the story Miu told me a few days ago in the village in Burgundy. It's not easy. She told the story in fits and starts, the chronology thoroughly mixed up. Sometimes I couldn't unravel which events happened first, and which came later, what was cause, what was effect. I don't blame her, though. The cruel conspiratorial razor buried in her memory slashed out at her, and as the stars faded with the dawn above the vineyard, so the life force drained from her cheeks as she told me her tale.

Miu told the story only after I insisted on hearing it. I had to run through a whole gamut of appeals to get her to talk – alternately encouraging her, bullying her, indulging, praising, enticing her to continue. We drank red wine and talked till dawn. Hands clasped together we followed the traces of her memories, piecing them together, analysing the results. Still there were places Miu couldn't dredge up from her memory. Once she dipped her foot there she grew quietly confused, and downed more wine. These were the danger zones of memory. Whenever we came across these, we'd give up the search and gingerly withdraw to higher ground.

I persuaded Miu to tell me the story after I became aware that she dyed her hair. Miu is such a careful person that only a very few people around her have any idea she dyes her hair. But I noticed it. Travelling together for so long, spending each day together, you tend to pick up on things like that. Or maybe Miu wasn't trying to hide it. She could have been much more discreet if she'd wanted to. Maybe she thought it was inevitable I'd find out, or maybe she *wanted* me to find out. (Hmm – pure conjecture on my part.)

I asked her straight out. That's me – never beat about the bush. How much of your hair is white? I asked. How long have you been dyeing it? Fourteen years, she answered. Fourteen years ago my hair turned entirely white, every single strand. Were you sick? No, that wasn't it, said Miu. Something happened, and all my hair turned pure white. Overnight.

I'd like to hear the story, I said, imploring her. I want to know everything about you. You know I wouldn't hide a thing from *you*. But Miu quietly shook her head. She'd never once told anyone the story; even her husband didn't know what had happened. For fourteen years it had been her own private secret.

But in the end we talked all night. Every story has a time to be told, I convinced her. Otherwise you'll be forever a prisoner to the secret inside you.

Miu looked at me as if gazing at some far-off scene. Something floated to the surface of her eyes, then slowly settled to the bottom again. "I have nothing I have to clear up," she said. "*They* have accounts to settle – not me."

I couldn't understand what she was driving at.

"If I do tell you the story," Miu said, "the two of us will always share it. And I don't know if that's the right thing to do. If I lift open the lid now, you'll be implicated. Is that what you want? You really want to know something I've sacrificed so much trying to forget?"

Yes, I said. No matter what it is, I want to share it with you. I don't want you to hide a thing.

Obviously confused, Miu took a sip of wine and closed her eyes. A silence followed in which time itself seemed to bend and buckle.

In the end, though, she began to tell the story. Bit by bit, one fragment at a time. Some elements of the story took on a life of their own, while others never even quivered into being. There were the inevitable gaps and elisions, some of which themselves had their own special significance. My task now, as narrator, is to gather – ever so carefully – all these elements into a whole.

The Tale of Miu and the Ferris Wheel

One summer Miu stayed alone in a small town in Switzerland near the French border. She was 25 and lived in Paris, where she studied the piano. She came to this little town at her father's request to take care of some business negotiations. The business itself was a simple matter, basically just having dinner once with the other party and having him sign a contract. Miu liked the little town the first time she laid eyes on it. It was such a cosy, lovely place, with a lake and medieval castle beside it. She thought it would be fun to live there, and took the plunge. Besides, a music festival was being held in a nearby village, and if she rented a car she could attend every day.

She was lucky enough to find a furnished apartment on a short-term lease, a pleasant, tidy little building on top of a hill on the outskirts of town. The view was superb. Nearby was a place where she could practise piano. The rent wasn't cheap, but if she found herself strapped for cash she could always rely on her father to help out.

Thus Miu began her temporary but placid life in the town. She'd attend concerts at the music festival, take walks in the neighbourhood, and before long got to make a few acquaintances. She found a nice little restaurant and café that she began to frequent. Out of the window of her apartment she could see an amusement park outside town. There was a giant Ferris wheel in the park. Colourful boxes with doors forever wed to the huge wheel, all of which would slowly rotate through the sky. Once it reached its upward limit, it began to descend.

Naturally. Ferris wheels don't go anywhere. They go up, they come back down, a roundabout trip that, for some strange reason, most people find pleasant.

In the evenings the Ferris wheel was speckled with countless lights. Even after it shut down for the night and the amusement park closed, the wheel twinkled all night long, as if vying with the stars in the sky. Miu would sit near her window, listening to music on the radio, and gaze forever at the up-and-down motion of the Ferris wheel. Or, when it was stopped, at the monument-like stillness of it.

She got to know a man who lived in the town. A handsome, 50-ish Latin type. He was tall, with a thoroughly handsome nose and dark straight hair. He introduced himself to her at the café. Where are you from? he asked. I'm from Japan, she answered. And the two of them began talking. His name was Ferdinando. He was from Barcelona, and had moved here five years before to work in furniture design.

He spoke in a relaxed way, often joking. They chatted for a while, then said goodbye. Two days later they met each other at the same café. He was single, divorced, she found out. He told her he left Spain to begin a new life. Miu didn't have a very good impression of the man. She could sense he was trying to move in on her. She sniffed a hint of sexual desire, and it frightened her. She decided to avoid the café.

Still, she bumped into Ferdinando many times in town – often enough to make her feel he was following her. Perhaps it was just a silly delusion. It was a small town, so running across the same person wasn't so strange. Every time he saw her, he smiled broadly and said hello in a friendly way. Still, ever so slowly, Miu became irritated and uneasy. She started to see Ferdinando as a threat to her peaceful life. Like a dissonant cymbal at the beginning of a musical score, an ominous shadow began to cloud her pleasant summer.

Ferdinando, though, turned out to be just a glimpse of a greater shadow. After living there ten days, she started to feel a kind of impediment attaching itself to her life in the town. The thoroughly lovely, neat-as-a-pin town now seemed narrow-minded, self-righteous. The people were friendly and kind enough, but she started to feel an invisible prejudice against her as an Asian. The wine she drank in restaurants suddenly had a bad aftertaste. She found worms in the vegetables she bought. The performances at the music festival sounded listless. She couldn't concentrate on her music. Even her apartment, which she thought quite comfortable, began to look to her like a poorly decorated, squalid place. Everything lost its initial lustre. The ominous shadow spread. And she couldn't escape it.

The phone would ring at night, and she'd pick it up. "Allo?" she'd say. But the phone would go dead. This happened again and again. It had to be Ferdinando, she thought. But she had no proof. How would he know her number? The phone was an old model, and she couldn't just unplug it. She had trouble sleeping, and started taking sleeping pills. Her appetite had gone.

I've got to get out of here, she decided. But for some reason she couldn't fathom, she couldn't drag herself away from the town. She made up a list of reasons to stay. She'd already paid a month's rent, and bought a pass to the music festival. And she'd already let out her apartment in Paris for the summer. She couldn't just up and leave now, she told herself. And besides, nothing had actually happened. She hadn't been hurt in any real way, had she? No one had treated her badly. I must just be getting overly sensitive to things, she convinced herself.

One evening, about two weeks after she began living there, she dined out as usual at a nearby restaurant. After dinner she decided to enjoy the night air for a change, and took a long stroll. Lost in thought, she wandered from one street to the next. Before she realized it, she was at the entrance to the amusement park. The park with the Ferris wheel. The air was filled with lively music, the sound of carnival barkers, and children's happy shouts. The visitors were mostly families, and a few couples from town. Miu remembered her father taking her to an amusement park once when she was little. She could remember even now the scent of her father's tweed coat as they rode the whirling teacups. The whole time they were on the ride, she clung to her father's sleeve. To young Miu that odour was a sign of the far-off world of adults, a symbol of security. She found herself missing her father.

Just for fun, she bought a ticket and went inside the park. The place was filled with different little shops and stands – a shooting gallery, a snake show, a fortune-teller's booth. Crystal ball in front of her, the fortune-teller, a largish woman, beckoned to Miu: "Mademoiselle, come here, please. It's very important. Your fate is about to change." Miu just smiled and passed by.

She bought some ice-cream and sat on a bench to eat it, watching the people passing by. She felt herself far removed from the bustling crowds around her. A man started to talk to her in German. He was about 30, small, with blond hair and a moustache, the kind of man who'd look good in a uniform. She shook her head and smiled and pointed to her watch. "I'm waiting for somebody," she said in French. Her voice sounded

161

higher, and remote to her. The man said nothing further, grinned sheepishly, gave her a brief wave of the hand and was gone.

Miu stood up, and wandered around. Somebody was throwing darts and a balloon burst. A bear was stomping around in a dance. An organ played "The Blue Danube Waltz". She looked up, and saw the Ferris wheel leisurely turning through the air. It would be fun to see my apartment from the Ferris wheel, she suddenly thought, instead of the other way around. Fortunately she had a small pair of binoculars in her shoulder bag. She had left them in there since the last time she was at the music festival, where they came in handy for seeing the stage from her far-off seat on the lawn. They were light and strong enough. With these she should be able to see right into her room.

She went to buy a ticket at the booth in front of the Ferris wheel. "We'll be closing pretty soon, Mademoiselle," the ticket seller, an old man, told her. He looked down as he mumbled this, as if talking to himself. And he shook his head. "We're almost finished for the day. This will be the last ride. One time around and we're finished." White stubble covered his chin, his whiskers stained by tobacco smoke. He coughed. His cheeks were as red as if buffeted for years in a north wind.

"That's all right. Once is enough," Miu replied. She bought a ticket and stepped up on the platform. She was the only person waiting to board, and as far as she could make out, the little gondolas were all empty. Empty boxes swung idly through the air as they revolved, as if the world itself were fizzling out towards its end.

She got inside the red gondola, sat on the bench, while the old man came over, closed the door, and locked it from the outside. For safety's sake, no doubt. Like some ancient animal coming to life, the Ferris wheel clattered and began its ascent. The assorted throng of booths and attractions shrank below her. As they did, the lights of the city rose up before her. The lake was on her left-hand side, and she could see lights from excursion boats reflected gently on the surface of the water. The far-off mountainside was dotted with lights from tiny villages. Her chest tightened at the beauty of it all.

The area where she lived, on the hilltop, came into view. Miu focused her binoculars and searched for her apartment, but it wasn't easy to find. The Ferris wheel steadily rose higher and higher. She'd have to hurry. She swept the binoculars back and forth in a frantic search. But there were too many buildings that looked alike. The Ferris wheel reached the top, and began its downward turn. Finally she spotted the building. That's it! But somehow it had more windows than she remembered. Lots of people had their windows open to catch the summer breeze. She moved her binoculars from one window to the next, and finally located the second apartment from the right on the third floor. But by then the Ferris wheel was getting closer to ground level. The walls of other buildings got in the way. It was a shame – just a few more seconds and she could have seen right inside her place.

The Ferris wheel approached the ground, ever so slowly. She tried to open the door to get out, but it wouldn't budge. Of course – it was locked from the outside. She looked around for the old man in the ticket booth, but he was nowhere to be seen. The light in the booth was already out. She was about to call to someone, but there wasn't anyone to yell to. The Ferris wheel

163

began rising once more. What a mess, she thought. How could this happen? She sighed. Maybe the old man had gone to the toilet and missed the timing. She'd have to make one more circuit.

It's all right, she thought. The old man's forgetfulness would give her a second free spin on the wheel. This time for sure she'd spot her apartment. She grasped the binoculars firmly and stuck her face out of the window. Since she'd located the general area and position last time around, this time it was an easy task to spot her own room. The window was open, the light on. She hated to come back to a dark room, and had planned to come back straight after dinner.

It gave her a guilty feeling to look at her own room from so far away through the binoculars, as if she were peeking in on herself. But I'm not there, she assured herself. Of course not. There's a phone on the table. I'd really like to place a call to that phone. There's a letter I left on the table, too. I'd like to read it from here, Miu thought. But naturally she couldn't see that much detail.

Finally the Ferris wheel passed its zenith and began to descend. It had only gone down a short while when it suddenly stopped. She was thrown against the side of the car, banging her shoulder and nearly dropping the binoculars on the floor. The sound of the Ferris wheel motor ground to a halt, and everything was wrapped in an unearthly silence. All the lively background music she'd heard was gone. Most of the lights in the booths down below were out. She listened carefully, but heard only the faint sound of the wind and nothing more. Absolute stillness. No voices of carnival barkers, no children's happy shouts. At first

164

she couldn't grasp what had happened. And then it came to her: she'd been abandoned.

She leaned out of the half-open window, and looked down again. She realized how high up she was. Miu thought to yell out for help, but knew that no one would hear her. She was too high up, her voice too small.

Where could that old man have gone to? He must have been drinking. His face that colour, his breath, his thick voice – no mistake about it. He forgot all about putting me on the Ferris wheel and turned the machinery off. At this very moment he's probably getting pissed in some bar, having a beer or gin, getting even more drunk and forgetting what he's done. Miu bit her lip. I might not get out of here until tomorrow afternoon, she thought. Or maybe evening? When did the amusement park open for business? She had no idea.

Miu was dressed only in a light blouse and short cotton skirt, and though it was the middle of summer the Swiss night air was chilly. The wind had picked up. She leaned out of the window once more to look at the scene below. There were even fewer lights than before. The amusement park staff had finished for the day and gone home. There had to be a guard around somewhere. She took a deep breath and shouted for help at the top of her lungs. She listened. And yelled again. And again. No response.

She took a small notebook from her shoulder bag, and wrote on it in French: "I'm locked inside the Ferris wheel at the amusement park. Please help me." She dropped the note out of the window. The sheet flew off on the wind. The wind was blowing towards the town, so if she was lucky it might end up there. But if someone actually did pick it up and read

165

it, would he (or she) believe it? On another page, she wrote her name and address along with the message. That should be more believable. People might not take it for a joke then, but realize she was in serious trouble. She sent half the pages in her notebook flying out on the wind.

Suddenly she got an idea, took everything out of her wallet except a ten-franc note, and put a note inside: "A woman is locked inside the Ferris wheel up above you. Please help." She dropped the wallet out the window. It fell straight down towards the ground. She couldn't see where it fell, though, or hear the thud of it hitting the ground. She put the same kind of note inside her purse and dropped that as well.

Miu looked at her wristwatch. It was 10.30. She rummaged around inside her shoulder bag to see what else she could find. Some simple make-up and a mirror, her passport. Sunglasses. Keys to her rental car and her apartment. An army knife for peeling fruit. A small plastic bag with three crackers inside. A French paperback. She'd eaten dinner, so she wouldn't be hungry until morning. With the cool air, she wouldn't get too thirsty. And fortunately she didn't have to go to the toilet yet.

She sat down on the plastic bench, and leaned her head back against the wall. Regrets spun through her mind. Why had she come to the amusement park, and got on this Ferris wheel? After she left the restaurant she should have gone straight home. If only she had, she'd be taking a nice hot bath right now, snuggling into bed with a good book, as she always did. Why hadn't she done that? And why in the world would they hire a hopeless drunk like that old man?

The Ferris wheel creaked in the wind. She tried to close the window so the wind wouldn't get in, but it didn't give an inch.

She gave up and sat on the floor. I knew I should have brought a sweater, she thought. As she'd left her apartment she'd paused, wondering if she should drape a cardigan over her shoulders. But the summer evening had looked so pleasant, and the restaurant was only three blocks from her place. At that point walking to the amusement park and getting on the Ferris wheel were the furthest things from her mind. Everything had gone wrong.

To help her relax, she removed her wristwatch, her thin silver bracelet, and the seashell-shaped earrings and stored them in her bag. She curled up in a corner of the floor, and hoped she could just sleep till morning. Naturally she couldn't get to sleep. She was cold, and uneasy. An occasional gust of wind shook the gondola. She closed her eyes and mentally played a Mozart sonata in C minor, moving her fingers on an imaginary keyboard. For no special reason, she'd memorized this piece that she'd played when she was a child. Halfway through the second movement, though, her mind grew dim. And she fell asleep.

How long she slept, she didn't know. It couldn't have been long. She woke with a start, and for a minute had no idea where she was. Slowly her memory returned. That's right, she thought, I'm stuck inside a Ferris wheel at an amusement park. She pulled her watch out of her bag; it was after midnight. Miu slowly stood up. Sleeping in such a cramped position had made all her joints ache. She yawned a couple of times, stretched, and rubbed her wrists.

Knowing she wouldn't be able to get back to sleep for a while, she took the paperback out of her bag to take her mind off her troubles, and began reading where she'd left off. It was a new mystery she'd bought at a bookshop in town. Luckily, the lights on the Ferris wheel were left on all night. After she'd read a few pages, though, she realized she wasn't following the plot. Her eyes were following the lines all right, but her mind was miles away.

Miu gave up and shut the book. She looked at the night sky. A thin layer of clouds covered the sky, and she couldn't make out any stars. There was a dim sliver of moon. The lights cast her reflection clearly on the gondola's glass window. She stared at her face for a long time. When will this be over? she asked herself. Hang in there. Later on this will all be just a funny story you'll tell people. Imagine getting locked inside a Ferris wheel in an amusement park in Switzerland!

But it didn't become a funny story.

This is where the real story begins.

A little later, she picked up her binoculars and looked out at the window of her apartment. Nothing had changed. Well, what do you expect? she asked herself, and smiled.

She looked at the other windows in the building. It was past midnight, and almost everyone was asleep. Most of the windows were dark. A few people, though, were up, lights on in their apartments. People on the lower floors had taken the precaution of closing their curtains. Those on the upper floors didn't bother, and left their curtains open to catch the cool night breeze. Life within these rooms was quietly, and completely, open to view. (Who would ever imagine that someone looking in with binoculars was hidden away in a Ferris wheel in the middle of the night?) Miu wasn't very interested in peeking in on others' private lives, though. She found looking in her own empty room far more absorbing.

*

When she made one complete circuit of the windows and returned to her own apartment, she gasped. There was a naked man in her bedroom. At first she thought she had the wrong apartment. She moved the binoculars up and down, back and forth. But there was no mistake; it was her room all right. Her furniture, her flowers in the vase, her apartment's paintings hanging on the wall. The man was Ferdinando. No mistake about it. He was sitting on her bed, stark naked. His chest and stomach were hairy, and his long penis hung down flaccidly like some drowsy animal.

What could he be doing in my room? A thin sheen of sweat broke out on Miu's forehead. How did he get in? Miu couldn't understand it. She was angry at first, then confused. Next, a woman appeared in the window. She had on a short-sleeve white blouse and a short blue cotton skirt. A woman? Miu clutched the binoculars tighter and fixed her eyes on the scene.

What she saw was *herself*.

Miu's mind went blank. I'm right here, looking at my room through binoculars. And in that room is *me*. Miu focused and refocused the binoculars. But no matter how many times she looked, it was *her* inside the room. Wearing the exact same clothes she had on now. Ferdinando held her close and carried her to the bed. Kissing her, he gently undressed the Miu inside the room. He took off her blouse, undid her bra, pulled off her skirt, kissed the base of her neck as he caressed her breasts with his hands. After a while, he pulled off her panties with one hand, panties exactly the same as the ones she had on now. Miu couldn't breathe. What was happening?

Before she realized it, Ferdinando's penis was erect, as stiff as a rod. She'd never seen one so huge. He took Miu's hand,

and placed it on his penis. He caressed her and licked her from head to toe. He took his own sweet time. She didn't resist. She – the Miu in the apartment – let him do whatever he wanted, thoroughly enjoying the rising passion. From time to time she would reach out and caress Ferdinando's penis and balls and allow him to touch her everywhere.

Miu couldn't drag her gaze away from this strange sight. She felt sick. Her throat was so parched she couldn't swallow. She felt as if she was going to vomit. Everything was grotesquely exaggerated, menacing, like some medieval allegorical painting. This is what Miu thought: that they were deliberately showing her this scene. *They* know I'm watching. But still she couldn't pull her eyes away.

A blank.

Then what happened?

Miu didn't remember. Her memory came to an abrupt halt at this point.

"I can't recall," she said. She covered her face with her hands. "All I know is that it was a horrifying experience," she added quietly. "I was right here, and another me was over *there*. And that man – Ferdinando – was doing all kinds of things to me over there."

"What do you mean, all kinds of things?"

"I just can't remember. *All kinds of things*. With me locked inside the Ferris wheel, he did whatever he wanted – to the me over *there*. It's not like I was afraid of sex. There was a time when I enjoyed casual sex a lot. But that wasn't what I was seeing there. It was all meaningless and obscene, with only one goal in mind – to make me thoroughly polluted. Ferdinando used all

170

the tricks he knew to soil me with his thick fingers and mammoth penis – not that the *me* over there felt that this was making *her* dirty. And in the end it wasn't even Ferdinando any more.

Not Ferdinando any more? I stared at Miu. If it wasn't Ferdinando, then who was it?

I don't know. I can't recall. But in the end it wasn't Ferdinando any more. Or maybe from the beginning it wasn't him.

The next thing she knew, Miu was lying in a hospital bed, a white hospital gown covering her naked body. All her joints ached. The doctor explained what had happened. In the morning one of the workers at the amusement park had found the wallet she'd dropped and worked out what had happened. He got the Ferris wheel down and called an ambulance. Inside the gondola Miu was unconscious, collapsed in a heap. She looked like she was in shock, her pupils non-reactive. Her face and arms were covered with abrasions, her blouse bloody. They took her to the hospital for treatment. Nobody could work out how she'd got the injuries. Thankfully none of them would leave any lasting scars. The police hauled in the old man who ran the Ferris wheel for questioning, but he had no memory at all of giving her a ride just near closing time.

The next day some local policemen came to question her. She had trouble answering their questions. When they compared her face with her picture in her passport, they frowned, strange expressions on their faces like they'd swallowed something awful. Hesitantly, they asked her: "Mademoiselle, we're sorry to have to ask, but are you really 25?"

"I am," she replied, "just like it says in my passport." Why did they have to ask that?

A little while later, though, when she went to the bathroom

to wash her face, she understood. Every single hair on her head was white. Pure white, like freshly driven snow. At first she thought it was somebody else in the mirror. She spun around. But she was alone in the bathroom. She looked in the mirror once more. And the reality of it all came crashing down on her in that instant. The white-haired woman staring back at her was *herself*. She fainted and fell to the floor.

And Miu vanished.

"I was still on *this* side, here. But *another me*, maybe half of me, had gone over to the *other side*. Taking with it my black hair, my sexual desire, my periods, my ovulation, perhaps even the will to live. And the half that was left is the person you see here. I've felt this way for the longest time – that in a Ferris wheel in a small Swiss town, for a reason I can't explain, I was split in two for ever. For all I know this may have been some kind of transaction. It's not like something was stolen away from me, because it all still exists, on the *other side*. Just a single mirror separates us from the other side. But I can never cross the boundary of that single pane of glass. Never."

Miu nibbled at her fingernails.

"I guess *never* is too strong a word. Maybe someday, somewhere, we'll meet again, and merge back into one. A very important question remains unanswered, however. Which *me*, on *which* side of the mirror, is the *real* me? I have no idea. Is the real me the one who held Ferdinando? Or the one who detested him? I don't have the confidence to work that one out."

After the summer holidays were over, Miu didn't return to school. She abandoned her studies abroad and went back to Japan. And never again did she touch a keyboard. The strength to make music had left her, never to return. A year later her father died and she took over his company.

"Not being able to play the piano any more was definitely a shock, but I didn't brood about it. I had a faint idea that, sooner or later, it was bound to happen. One of these days . . ." Miu smiled. "The world is filled with pianists. Twenty active world-class pianists are more than enough. Go to a record shop and check out all the versions of the 'Waldstein', the 'Kreisleriana', whatever. There are only so many classical pieces to record, only so much space on the CD shelves at shops. As far as the recording industry's concerned, 20 top-notch pianists are plenty. No one was going to care if I wasn't one of them."

Miu spread her ten fingers out before her, and turned them over again and again, as if she were making sure of her memory.

"After I'd been in France for about a year I noticed a strange thing. Pianists whose technique was worse than mine, and who didn't practise nearly half as much as I did, were able to move their audiences more than I ever could. In the end they defeated me. At first I thought it was just a misunderstanding. But the same thing happened so many times it made me angry. It's so unfair! I thought. Slowly but surely, though, I understood – that something was missing from me. Something absolutely critical, though I didn't know what. The kind of depth of emotion a person needs to make music that will inspire others, I guess. I hadn't noticed this when I was in Japan. In Japan I never lost to anyone, and I certainly didn't have the time to criticize my own performance. But in Paris surrounded by so many talented pianists, I finally understood that. It was entirely clear – like when the sun rises and the fog melts away."

Miu sighed. She looked up and smiled.

"Ever since I was little I've enjoyed making my own private rules and living by them. I was a very independent, super-serious type of girl. I was born in Japan, went to Japanese schools, grew up playing with Japanese friends. Emotionally I was completely Japanese, but by nationality I was a foreigner. Technically speaking Japan will always be a foreign country. My parents weren't the kind to be strict about things, but that's one thing they drummed into my head since I can remember: You are a *foreigner* here. I decided that in order for me to survive I needed to make myself stronger."

Miu continued in a calm voice.

"Being tough isn't of itself a bad thing. Looking back on it, though, I can see I was too used to being strong, and never tried to understand those who were weak. I was too used to being fortunate, and didn't try to understand those less fortunate. Too used to being healthy, and didn't try to understand the pain of those who weren't. Whenever I saw a person in trouble, somebody paralysed by events, I decided it was entirely their fault – they just weren't trying hard enough. People who complain were just plain lazy. My outlook on life was unshakeable, and practical, but lacked any human warmth. And not a single person around me pointed this out.

"I lost my virginity at 17, and slept with quite a few men. I had a lot of boyfriends, and if the mood struck me, I didn't mind one-night stands. But never once did I truly love someone. I didn't have the time. All I could think about was becoming a world-class pianist, and deviating from that path was not an option. Something was missing in me, but by the time I noticed that gap, it was too late."

Again she spread out both hands in front of her, and thought for a while.

"In that sense, what happened in Switzerland 14 years ago may well have been something I created myself. Sometimes I believe that."

Miu married at 29. Ever since the incident in Switzerland, she was totally frigid, and couldn't manage sex with anyone. Something inside her had vanished for ever. She shared this fact – and this fact alone – with the man she ended up marrying. That's why I can't marry anyone, she explained. But the man loved Miu, and even if it meant a platonic relationship, he wanted to share the rest of his life with her. Miu couldn't come up with a valid reason for turning down his proposal. She'd known him since she was a child, and had always been fond of him. No matter what form the relationship might take, he was the only person she could picture sharing her life with. Also, on the practical side, being married was important as far as carrying on her family business was concerned.

Miu continued.

"My husband and I see each other only at weekends, and generally get along well. We're like good friends, life partners able to pass some pleasant time together. We talk about all sorts of things, and we trust each other implicitly. Where and how he has a sex life I don't know, and I don't really care. We never make love, though – never even touch each other. I feel bad about it, but I don't want to touch him. I just don't want to."

Worn out with talking, Miu quietly covered her face with her hands. Outside, the sky had turned light.

"I was alive in the past, and I'm alive now, sitting here talking to you. But what you see here isn't really me. This is just a shadow of who I was. *You* are really living. But I'm not. Even these words I'm saying right now sound empty, like an echo."

Wordlessly I put my arm around Miu's shoulder. I couldn't find the right words, so I just held her.

I'm in love with Miu. With the Miu on *this side*, needless to say. But I also love the Miu on the other side just as much. The moment this thought struck me it was like I could hear myself – with an audible creak – splitting in two. As if Miu's own split became a rupture that had taken hold of me. The feeling was overpowering, and I knew there was nothing I could do to fight it.

One question remains, however. If *this* side, where Miu is, is not the real world – if *this* side is actually the *other* side – what about me, the person who shares the same temporal and spatial plane with her?

Who in the world am *I*?

13

I read both documents twice, a quick run-through at first, then slowly, paying attention to the details, engraving them on my mind. The documents were definitely Sumire's; the writing was filled with her one-of-a-kind phrasing. There was something different about the overall tone, though, something I couldn't pin down. It was more restrained, more distanced. Still, there was no doubt about it – Sumire had written both.

After a moment's hesitation, I slipped the floppy disk into the pocket of my bag. If Sumire were to come back without incident, I'd just put it back where it belonged. The problem was what to do if she *didn't* return. If somebody went through her belongings, they were bound to find the disk, and I couldn't abide the thought of other eyes prying into what I had just read.

After I read the documents, I had to get out of the house. I changed into a new shirt, left the cottage, and clambered down the staircase to town. I exchanged $100-worth of traveller's cheques, bought an English-language tabloid at the kiosk, and sat under a parasol at a café, reading. A sleepy waiter took my order for lemonade and melted cheese on toast. He wrote down the order with a stubby pencil, in no particular hurry. Sweat had seeped through the back of his shirt, forming a large stain. The stain seemed to be sending out a message, but I couldn't decipher it.

I mechanically leafed through half the paper, then gazed absently at the harbour scene. A skinny black dog came out of nowhere, sniffed my legs, then, losing interest, padded away. People passed the languid summer afternoon, each in his own personal spot. The only ones who seemed to be moving were the waiter and the dog, though I had my doubts about how long they'd keep at it. The old man at the kiosk where I'd bought the paper had been fast asleep under a parasol, legs spread wide apart. The statue of the hero in the square stood impassively as always, back turned to the intense sunlight.

I cooled my palms and forehead with the cold glass of lemonade, turning over and over in my mind any connections there might be between Sumire's disappearance and what she'd written.

For a long time Sumire had not written. When she first met Miu at the wedding reception, her desire to write had flown out of the window. Still, here on this little island, she'd managed those two pieces in a short space of time. No mean feat to complete that much in a few days. Something must have driven Sumire to sit at her desk and write. Where was the motivation?

More to the point, what theme tied these two pieces

of writing together? I looked up, gazed at the birds resting on the wharf, and gave it some thought.

It was far too hot to think about complicated matters. Admittedly I was confused and tired. Still, as if marshalling together the remnants of a defeated army – minus any drums and trumpets – I rallied my scattered thoughts. My mind focused, I began to piece it together.

"What's really important here," I whispered aloud to myself, "is not the big things other people have thought up, but the small things you, yourself, have." My standard maxim I taught my own students. But was it really true? It's easy to say, but putting it into practice isn't. One's hard put to start with even the small things, let alone the Big Picture. Or maybe the smaller the notion, the harder it is to grasp? Plus it didn't help that I was so far from home.

Sumire's dream. Miu's split.

These are two different worlds, I realized. *That's* the common element here.

Document 1: This relates a dream Sumire had. She's climbing a long staircase to go to see her dead mother. But the moment she arrives, her mother is already returning to the other side. And Sumire can't stop her. And she's left standing on the spire of a tower, surrounded by objects from a different world. Sumire's had many similar dreams.

Document 2: This one concerns the strange experiences Miu had 14 years ago. She was stuck inside a Ferris wheel overnight in an amusement park in a small Swiss town, and looking through binoculars at her own room she saw a second self there. A doppelgänger. And this experience destroyed Miu as a person – or at least made this destruction tangible. As Miu put it, she was split in two, with a mirror in between each self. Sumire had persuaded Miu to tell the story and wrote it down as best she could.

This side – the other side. That was the common thread. The movement from one side to the other. Sumire must have been drawn by this motif and motivated enough to spend so much time writing it all down. To borrow her own word, writing all this helped her *think*.

The waiter came to clear away the remnants of my toast, and I ordered a refill of lemonade. "Put in lots of ice," I asked him. When he brought the drink over I took a sip and used it again to cool my forehead.

"And if Miu doesn't accept me, then what?" Sumire had written. "I'll cross that bridge when the times comes. Blood must be shed. I'll sharpen my knife, ready to slit a dog's throat somewhere."

What was she trying to convey? Was she hinting that she might kill herself? I couldn't believe that. Her words didn't have the acrid smell of death. What I sensed in them was rather the will to move forwards, the struggle to make a new start. Dogs and blood are just metaphors, like I'd explained to her on that bench at Inogashira Park. They get their meaning from magical, life-giving forces. The story about the Chinese gates was a metaphor of how a story captures that magic.

Ready to slit a dog's throat somewhere.

Somewhere?

My thoughts slammed into a solid wall. A total dead end.

Where could Sumire have gone to? Is there somewhere she had to go to on this island?

I couldn't shake the image of Sumire falling down a well in some remote area and waiting, alone, for help to arrive. Injured, lonely, starving, and thirsty. The thought of this nearly drove me crazy.

The police had made clear that there wasn't a single well on the island. They'd never heard of any holes either anywhere near town. If there were, we'd be the first to know, they declared. I had to grant them that.

I decided to venture a theory.

Sumire went over to the *other side*.

That would explain a lot. Sumire broke through the mirror and journeyed to the other side. To meet the other Miu who was there. If the Miu on this side rejected her, wouldn't that be the logical thing to do?

I dredged up from memory what she'd written: "So what should we do to avoid a collision? Logically, it's easy. The answer is *dreams*. Dreaming on and on. Entering the world of dreams, and never coming out. Living there for the rest of time."

One question remains, however. A major question. How are you supposed to go there?

Put in simple logical terms, it's easy. Though explaining it isn't.

I was right back where I started.

I thought about Tokyo. About my apartment, the school where I taught, the kitchen rubbish I'd steathily tossed in

181

a bin at the station. I'd only been away from Japan for two days, but already it seemed like a different world. The new term was going to start in a week. I pictured myself standing in front of 35 pupils. Seen from this distance, the thought of my teaching anyone – even ten-year-old kids – seemed absurd.

I removed my sunglasses, wiped my sweating brow with a handkerchief, and put them on again, then gazed at the seabirds.

I thought about Sumire. About the colossal hard-on I had the time I sat beside her when she moved into her new place. The kind of awesome, rock-hard erection I'd never experienced before. Like my whole body was about to explode. At the time, in my imagination – something like the *world of dreams* Sumire wrote of – I made love to her. And the sensation was far more real than any sex I'd ever had.

I gulped down some lemonade to clear my throat.

I returned to my hypothesis, taking it one step further. Sumire had somehow found an exit. What kind of exit that was, and how she discovered it, I had no way of knowing. I'll put that on hold. Suppose it's a kind of door. I closed my eyes and conjured up a mental image – an elaborate image of what this door looked like. Just an ordinary door, part of an ordinary wall. Sumire happened to find this door, turned the knob, and slipped outside – from *this* side to the *other*. Clad only in thin silk pyjamas and a pair of flip-flops.

What lay beyond that door was beyond my powers of imagination. The door closed, and Sumire wouldn't be coming back.

I went back to the cottage and made a simple dinner from things I found in the fridge. Tomato and basil pasta, a salad, an Amstel beer. I went out to sit on the veranda, lost in thought. Or maybe thinking of nothing. Nobody phoned. Miu might be trying to call from Athens, but you couldn't count on the phones to work.

Moment by moment the blue of the sky turned deeper, a large circular moon rising from the sea, a handful of stars piercing holes in the sky. A breeze blew up the slopes, rustling the hibiscus. The unmanned lighthouse at the tip of the pier blinked on and off with its ancient-looking light. People were slowly heading down the slope, leading donkeys as they went. Their loud conversation came closer, then faded into the distance. I silently took it all in, this foreign scene seeming entirely natural.

In the end the phone didn't ring, and Sumire didn't appear. Quietly, gently, time slipped by, the evening deepening. I took a couple of cassettes from Sumire's room and played them on the living room stereo. One of them was a collection of Mozart songs. The handwritten label read: *Elisabeth Schwarzkopf and Walter Gieseking (p)*. I don't know much about classical music, but one listen told me how lovely this music was. The singing style was a bit dated, but it reminded me of reading some beautiful, memorable prose – it demanded that you sit up straight and pay attention. The performers were right there in front of me, it seemed, their delicate phrasing swelling up, then retreating, then swelling up again. One of the songs in the collection must be "Sumire". I sank back in my chair, closed my eyes, and shared this music with my missing friend.

I was awakened by music. Far-off music, barely audible. Steadily, like a faceless sailor hauling in an anchor from the bottom of the sea, the faint sound brought me to my senses. I sat up in bed, leaned towards the open window, and listened carefully. It was definitely music. The wristwatch next to my bed showed it was past one o'clock. Music? At this time of night?

I put on my trousers and a shirt, slipped on my shoes, and went outside. The lights in the neighbourhood were all out, the streets deserted. No wind, not even the sound of waves. Just the moonlight bathing the earth. I stood there, listening again. Strangely, the music seemed to be coming from the top of the hills. There weren't any villages on the steep mountains, just a handful of shepherds and monasteries where monks lived their cloistered lives. It was hard to imagine either group putting on a festival at this time of night.

Outside, the music was more audible. I couldn't make out the melody, but by the rhythm it was clearly Greek. It had the uneven, sharp sound of live music, not something played through speakers.

By then I was wide awake. The summer night air was pleasant, with a mysterious depth to it. If I hadn't been worried about Sumire, I might very well have felt a sense of celebration. I rested my hands on my hips, stretched, looking up at the sky, and took a deep breath. The coolness of the night washed inside me. Suddenly a thought struck me – maybe, at this very moment, Sumire is listening to the same music.

I decided to walk for a while in the direction of the sound. I had to find out where it was coming from, who was playing it. The road to the hilltop was the same one I'd taken that morning to go to the beach, so I knew the way. I'll go as far as I can, I decided.

The brilliant moonlight lit everything, making walking easy. It created complex shadows between the cliffs, dyeing the ground with unlikely shades. Every time the soles of my running shoes crushed a pebble on the road, the sound was amplified. The music grew more pronounced as I made my way further up the slopes. As I'd surmised, it was coming from the top of the hill. I could make out some kind of percussion instrument, a bouzouki, an accordion, and a flute. Possibly a guitar. Other than that, I couldn't hear a thing. No singing, no people shouting. Just that music playing endlessly, at a detached, almost monotonous pace.

I wanted to see what was taking place on top of the mountain, yet at the same time I thought I should keep my distance. Irrepressible curiosity vied with an instinctive fear. Still, I had to go forward. I felt as if I was in a dream. The principle that made other choices possible was missing. Or was it the choice that made that principle possible that was missing?

For all I knew, a few days before Sumire had awakened to the same music, her curiosity getting the better of her as she clambered up the slope in her pyjamas.

I stopped and turned to look behind me. The slope twisted palely down towards the town like the tracks of some gigantic insect. I looked up at the sky then, under the moonlight, and glanced at my palm. With a rush of understanding

I knew this wasn't my hand any more. I can't explain it. But at a glance I *knew*. My hand was no longer my hand, my legs no longer my legs.

Bathed in the pallid moonlight, my body, like some plaster puppet, had lost all living warmth. As if a voodoo magician had put a spell on me, blowing my transient life into this lump of clay. The spark of life had vanished. My real life had fallen asleep somewhere, and a faceless someone was stuffing it in a suitcase, about to leave.

An awful chill swept through me and I felt choked. Someone had rearranged my cells, untied the threads that held my mind together. I couldn't think straight. All I was able to do was retreat as fast as I could to my usual place of refuge. I took a huge breath, sinking in the sea of consciousness to the very bottom. Pushing aside the heavy water I plunged down quickly and grabbed a huge rock there with both arms. The water crushed my eardrums. I squeezed my eyes tightly closed, held my breath, resisting. Once I made up my mind, it wasn't that difficult. I grew used to it all – the water pressure, the lack of air, the freezing darkness, the signals the chaos emitted. It was something I'd mastered again and again as a child.

Time reversed itself, looped back, collapsed, reordered itself. The world stretched out endlessly – and yet was defined and limited. Sharp images – just the images alone – passed down dark corridors, like jellyfish, like souls adrift. But I steeled myself not to look at them. If I acknowledged them, even a little, they would envelop themselves in meaning. Meaning was fixed to the temporal, and the temporal was trying to force me to rise to the surface. I shut my mind tight to it all, waiting for the procession to pass.

How long I remained that way, I don't know. When I bobbed to the surface, opened my eyes, and took a silent breath, the music had already stopped. The enigmatic performance was finished. I listened carefully. I couldn't hear a thing. Absolutely nothing. No music, no people's voices, no rustle of the wind.

I tried to check the time, but I wasn't wearing a watch. I'd left it by my bedside.

The sky was now filled with stars. Or was it my imagination? The sky itself seemed to have changed into something different. The strange sense of alienation I'd felt inside had vanished. I stretched, bent my arm, my fingers. No sense of being out of place. My underarms were clammy, but that was all.

I stood up from the grass and continued to climb uphill. I'd come this far and might as well reach the top. Had there really been music there? I had to see for myself, even if only the faintest clues remained. In five minutes I reached the summit. Towards the south the hill sloped down to the sea, the harbour, and the sleeping town. A scattering of streetlights lit the coast road. The other side of the mountain was wrapped in darkness, not a single light visible. I gazed fixedly into the dark, and finally a line of hills beyond floated into sight in the moonlight. Beyond them lay an even deeper darkness. And here around me, no indication whatsoever that a lively festival had taken place only a short while before.

Though the echo of it remained deep inside my head, now I wasn't even sure I'd heard music. As time passed, I became less and less certain. Maybe it had all been an illusion, my ears picking up signals from a different time and place. It made sense – the idea that people would get together on a mountaintop at 1 a.m. to play music *was* pretty preposterous.

In the sky above the summit, the coarse-looking moon loomed awfully near. A hard ball of stone, its skin eaten away by the merciless passage of time. Ominous shadows on its surface were blind cancer cells stretching out feelers towards the warmth of life. The moonlight warped every sound, washed away all meaning, threw every mind into chaos. It made Miu see a second self. It took Sumire's cat away somewhere. It made Sumire disappear. And it brought me here, in the midst of music that – most likely – never existed. Before me lay a bottomless darkness; behind me, a world of pale light. I stood there on the top of a mountain in a foreign land, bathed in moonlight. Maybe this had all been meticulously planned, from the very beginning.

I returned to the cottage and downed a glass of Miu's brandy. I tried to get to sleep, but I couldn't. Not a wink. Until the eastern sky grew light, I was held in the grip of the moon, and gravity, and something astir in the world.

I pictured cats, starving to death in a closed-up apartment. Soft, small carnivores. I – the *real* me – was dead, and they were alive, devouring my flesh, chewing on my heart, sucking my blood. If I listened very carefully, somewhere far, far away I could hear the cats lapping up my brain. Three lithe cats, surrounding my broken head, slurping up the mushy grey soup within. The tips of their red, rough tongues licked the soft folds of my mind. And with each lick of their tongues, my mind – like a shimmer of hot air – flickered and faded away.

14

In the end we never found out what happened to Sumire. As Miu put it, she vanished like smoke.

Two days later Miu came back to the island on the noon ferry together with an official from the Japanese embassy and a police official in charge of tourist affairs. They met with the local police and launched a full-scale investigation involving the islanders. The police put out a public appeal for information, publishing a blown-up version of Sumire's passport photo in a national newspaper. Many people got in touch, but nothing connected. The information always turned out to be about someone else.

Sumire's parents came to the island, too. I left just before they arrived. The new school term was around the corner, but mostly I couldn't stand the thought of facing them. Besides, the mass media in Japan had caught wind of events and had begun to contact the Japanese embassy and the local police. I told Miu it was about time for me to be getting back to Tokyo. Staying any longer on the island wasn't going to help find Sumire.

She nodded. "You've done so much already," she said. "Really. If you hadn't come, I would have been completely lost. Don't worry. I'll explain things to Sumire's parents. And I'll handle any reporters. Leave it to me. You had no responsibility for any of this to begin with. I can be pretty businesslike when I need to be, and I can hold my own."

She saw me off at the harbour. I was taking the afternoon ferry to Rhodes. It was exactly ten days since Sumire had disappeared. Miu hugged me just before I left. A very natural embrace. For a long moment, she silently rubbed my back as she held me. The afternoon sun was hot, but strangely her skin felt cool. Her hand was trying to tell me something. I closed my eyes and listened to those words. Not words – something that couldn't coalesce into language. In the midst of our silence, something passed between us.

"Take care of yourself," said Miu.

"You, too," I said. For a while we stood there in front of the gangplank.

"I want you to tell me something, honestly," She said in a serious tone, just before I boarded the ferry. "Do you believe Sumire is no longer alive?"

I shook my head. "I can't prove it, but I feel like she's still alive somewhere. Even after this much time, I just don't have the sense that she's dead."

Miu folded her tanned arms and looked at me.

"Actually I feel exactly the same," she said. "That Sumire isn't dead. But I also feel that I'll never see her again. Though I can't prove anything either."

I didn't say a word. Silence wove itself into the spaces of everything around us. Seabirds squawked as they cut across the cloudless sky, and in the café the ever-sleepy waiter hoisted yet another tray of drinks.

Miu pursed her lips and was lost in thought. "Do you hate me?" she finally asked.

"Because Sumire disappeared?"

"Yes."

"Why would I hate you?"

"I don't know." Her voice was tinged with a long-suppressed exhaustion. "I have the feeling I'll never see you again, either. That's why I asked."

"I don't hate you," I said.

"But who can tell, maybe later on?"

"I don't hate people over things like that."

Miu took off her hat, straightened her fringe, and put it back on. She squinted at me.

"That might be because you don't expect anything from anyone," she said. Her eyes were deep and clear, like the twilit darkness on the day we met. "I'm not like that. I just want you to know that I like you. Very much."

And we said goodbye. The ship edged backwards out of the harbour, the propeller churning up the water as it lumbered through a 180° change of direction; all the while, Miu stood on the wharf watching me go. She wore a tight white dress and occasionally reached out to keep her hat from flying away in the wind. Standing there on that wharf on this little Greek island, she looked like something from a different world, fleeting, full of grace and beauty. I leaned against the railing on deck and watched her for a long time.

191

Time seemed to stand still, the scene forever etched on my memory.

But time began to move again, and Miu got smaller and smaller, first a vague dot, then swallowed up whole in the shimmering air. The town grew distant, the shape of the mountains indistinct, and finally the island merged into the mist of light, blurred, and vanished altogether. Another island rose up to take its place and likewise disappeared into the distance. As time passed, all the things I left behind there seemed never to have existed at all.

Maybe I should have stayed with Miu. So what if the new school term was starting? I should encourage Miu, do everything I could to help in the search, and if something awful happened, then I should hold her, give her what comfort I could. Miu wanted me, I believe, and in a sense I wanted her as well.

She'd grabbed hold of my heart with a rare intensity.

I realized all this for the first time as I stood on the deck and watched her disappear in the distance. A feeling came over me, like a thousand strings were tugging at me. Perhaps not full-blown romantic love, but something very close. Flustered, I sat on a bench on the deck, placed my gym bag on my knees, and gazed out at the white wake trailing behind the ship. Seagulls flew after the ferry, clinging to the wake. I could still feel Miu's small palm on my back, like a soul's tiny shadow.

I planned to fly straight back to Tokyo, but for some reason the reservation I'd made the day before was cancelled, and I ended up spending the night in Athens. I took the airline shuttle bus and stayed at a hotel in the city that the airline recommended. A pleasant, cosy hotel near the Plaka district, which, unfortunately, was crowded with a boisterous German tour group. With nothing else to do, I wandered around the city, bought some souvenirs for no one in particular, and in the evening walked to the top of the Acropolis. I lay down on a slab of stone, the twilight breeze blowing over me as I gazed at the white temple floating up in the bluish floodlights. A lovely, dreamy scene.

But all I felt was an incomparable loneliness. Before I knew it, the world around was drained of colour. From the shabby mountaintop, the ruins of those empty feelings, I could see my own life stretching out into the future. It looked just like an illustration in a science fiction novel I read as a child: the desolate surface of a deserted planet. No sign of life at all. Each day seemed to last for ever, the air either boiling hot or freezing. The spaceship that brought me there had disappeared, and I was stuck. I'd have to survive on my own.

All over again I understood how important, how irreplaceable, Sumire was to me. In her own special way she'd kept me tethered to the world. As I talked to her and read her stories, my mind quietly expanded, and I could see things I'd never seen before. Without even trying, we grew close. Like a pair of young lovers undressing in front of each other, Sumire and I had exposed our hearts to one another, an experience I'd never have with anyone else, anywhere. We cherished what we had together, though we never put into words how very precious it was.

Of course it hurt that we could never love each other in a physical way. We would have been far happier if we had. But that was like the tides, the change of seasons – something immutable, an immovable destiny we could never alter. No matter how cleverly we might shelter it, our delicate friendship wasn't going to last for ever. We were bound to reach a dead end. That was painfully clear.

I loved Sumire more than anyone else and wanted her more than anything in the world. And I couldn't just shelve those feelings, for there was nothing to take their place.

I dreamed that someday there'd be a sudden, major *transformation*. Even if the chances of it coming true were slim, I could dream about it, couldn't I? But I knew it would never come true.

Like the tide receding, the shoreline washed clean, with Sumire gone I was left in a distorted, empty world. A gloomy, cold world in which what she and I had would never ever take place again.

We each have a special *something* we can get only at a special time of our life. Like a small flame. A careful, fortunate few cherish that flame, nurture it, hold it as a torch to light their way. But once that flame goes out, it's gone for ever. What I'd lost was not just Sumire. I'd lost that precious flame.

What is it like – on *the other side*? Sumire was over there, and so was the lost part of Miu. Miu with black hair and a healthy sexual appetite. Perhaps they've come across each other there, loving each other, fulfilling each other. "We do things you can't put into words," Sumire would probably tell me, putting it into words all the same.

*

Is there a place for me over there? Could I be with them? While they make passionate love, I'd sit in the corner of a room somewhere and amuse myself reading the *Collected Works* of Balzac. After she showered, Sumire and I would take long walks and talk about all kinds of things – with Sumire, as usual, doing most of the talking. But would our relationship last for ever? Is that natural? "Of course," Sumire would tell me. "No need to ask that. 'Cause you're my one and only true friend!"

But I hadn't a clue how to get to that world. I rubbed the slick, hard rock face of the Acropolis. History had seeped through the surface and was stored up inside. Like it or not, I was shut up in that flow of time. I couldn't escape. No – that's not entirely true. The truth is, I really don't want to escape.

Tomorrow I'll get on a plane and fly back to Tokyo. The summer holidays are nearly over, and I have to step once more in that endless stream of the everyday. There's a place for me there. My apartment's there, my desk, my class-room, my pupils. Quiet days await me, novels to read. The occasional affair.

But tomorrow I'll be a different person, never again the person I was. Not that anyone will notice after I'm back in Japan. On the outside nothing will be different. But something inside has burned up and vanished. Blood has been shed, and something inside me is gone. Face turned down, without a word, that *something* makes its exit. The door opens; the door shuts. The light goes out. This is the last day for the person I am right now. The very last twilight.

When dawn comes, the person I am won't be here any more. Someone else will occupy this body.

Why do people have to be this lonely? What's the point of it all? Millions of people in this world, all of them yearning, looking to others to satisfy them, yet isolating themselves. Why? Was the Earth put here just to nourish human loneliness?

I turned face-up on the slab of stone, gazed at the sky, and thought about all the man-made satellites spinning around the Earth. The horizon was still etched in a faint glow, and stars began to blink on in the deep, wine-coloured sky. I gazed among them for the light of a satellite, but it was still too bright out to spot one with the naked eye. The sprinkling of stars looked nailed to the spot, unmoving. I closed my eyes and listened carefully for the descendants of Sputnik, even now circling the Earth, gravity their only tie to the planet. Lonely metal souls in the unimpeded darkness of space, they meet, pass each other, and part, never to meet again. No words passing between them. No promises to keep.

15

The phone rang on a Sunday afternoon. The second Sunday after the new school term began in September. I was fixing a late lunch and had to turn off the gas range before I answered. The phone rang with a kind of urgency – at least it felt that way. I was sure it was Miu calling with news of Sumire's whereabouts. The call wasn't from Miu, though, but from my girlfriend.

"Something's happened," she said, skipping her usual opening pleasantries. "Can you come straightaway?"

It sounded like something awful. Had her husband found out about us? I took a deep breath. If people discovered I was sleeping with the mother of one of the kids in my class, I'd be in a major fix to say the least. Worst-case scenario, I could lose my job. At the same time, though, I was resigned to it. I knew the risks.

"Where are you?" I asked.

"At a supermarket," she said.

I took the train to Tachikawa, arriving at the station near the supermarket at 2.30. The afternoon was blazing hot, the summer back in force, but I had on a white dress-shirt, tie, and light grey suit, the clothes she'd asked me to wear. "You look more like a teacher that way," she said, "and you'll give a better impression. Sometimes you still look like a college student," she added.

At the entrance to the supermarket I asked a young assistant who was rounding up stray shopping trolleys where the security office was. He told me it was across the street on the third floor of an annexe, an ugly little three-storey building without even a lift. Hey, don't worry about us, the cracks in the concrete walls seemed to say, They're just going to tear this place down someday anyway. I walked up the narrow, timeworn stairs, located the door with SECURITY on it, and gave a couple of light taps. A man's deep voice answered. I opened the door and saw my girlfriend and her son inside seated in front of a desk facing a middle-aged uniformed security guard. Just the three of them.

The room was an in-between size, not too big, not too small. Three desks were lined up along the window, a steel locker against the wall opposite. On the wall between were a duty rota and three security guard caps on a steel shelf. Beyond a frosted-glass door at the far end of the room there seemed to be a second room, which the guards probably used for taking naps. The room we were all in was almost completely devoid of decoration. No flowers, no pictures, not even a calendar. Just an overly large round clock on the wall. A totally barren room, like some ancient corner of the world that time forgot. On top of which the place had a strange odour – of cigarette smoke, mouldy documents, and perspiration mixed together over the years.

The security guard in charge was a thickset man in his late fifties. He had beefy arms and a large head covered with a thick patch of coarse salt-and-pepper hair he'd plastered down with some cheap hair tonic, the best he could probably afford on his lowly security guard salary. The ashtray in front of him was overflowing with Seven Star butts. When I came in the room, he took off his black-framed glasses, wiped them with a cloth, and put them back on. Maybe his set way of greeting new people. With his glasses off, his eyes were as cold as moon rocks. When he put them back on, the coldness retreated, replaced by a kind of powerful glazed look. Either way, this wasn't a look to put people at their ease.

The room was oppressively hot; the window was wide open, but not a breath of air came in. Only the noise from the road outside. A large lorry coming to a halt at a red light blatted out a hoarse air brake, reminding me of Ben Webster on the tenor sax in his later years. We were all sweating. I walked up to the desk, introduced myself, and handed the security guard my business card. He took it without a word, pursed his lips, and stared at it for a while, then placed it on the desk and looked up at me.

"You're pretty young for a teacher, aren't you?" he said. "How long have you been teaching?"

I pretended to think it over and answered, "Three years."

"Hmm," he said. And didn't say anything else. But the silence spoke volumes. He picked up my card and read my name again, as if re-checking something.

"My name's Nakamura, I'm the chief of security here," he introduced himself. He didn't proffer a business card of his own. "Just pull up a chair from over there if you would. I'm sorry about how hot it is. The air conditioner's on the blink, and no one will come out to fix it on a Sunday. They aren't nice enough to give me a fan, so I sit and suffer. Take off your jacket if you'd like. We might be here for a while, and it makes me hot just looking at you."

I did as he told me, pulling over a chair and removing my jacket. My sweaty shirt clung to my skin.

"You know, I've always envied teachers," the guard began. A stillborn smile played around his lips, yet his eyes remained those of a deep-sea predator searching my depths for the slightest movement. His words were polite enough, but that was only a veneer. The word *teacher* sounded like an insult.

"You have over a month off in the summer, don't have to work on Sundays or at night, and people give you gifts all the time. Pretty nice life if you ask me. I sometimes wish I'd studied harder and become a teacher myself. Destiny intervened and here I am – a security guard at a supermarket. I wasn't smart enough, I suppose. But I tell my kids to grow up to be teachers. I don't care what anybody says, teachers have it made."

My girlfriend wore a simple blue, half-sleeve dress. Her hair was piled up neatly on top of her head, and she had on a pair of small earrings. White sandals with heels completed her outfit, and a white bag and small, cream-coloured hand-kerchief rested on her lap. It was the first time I'd seen her since I got back from Greece. She looked back and forth between me and the guard, her eyes puffy from crying. She'd been through a lot, it was clear.

We exchanged a quick glance, and I turned to her son. His name was Shin'ichi Nimura, but his classmates nicknamed him Carrot. With his long, thin face, his shock of unkempt, curly hair, the name fitted. I usually called him that, too. He was a quiet boy, hardly ever speaking more than was necessary. His grades weren't bad; he rarely forgot to bring his homework and never failed to do his share of the cleaning up. Never got into trouble. But he lacked initiative and never once raised his hand in class. Carrot's classmates didn't dislike him, but he wasn't what you'd call popular. This didn't please his mother much, but from my point of view he was a good kid.

"I assume you've heard about what happened from the boy's mother," the security guard said.

"Yes, I have," I replied. "He was caught shoplifting."

"That's correct," the guard said and set a cardboard box that was at his feet on top of the table. He pushed it towards me. Inside was a collection of identical small staplers still in their packaging. I picked one up and examined it. The price tag said ¥850.

"Eight staplers," I commented. "Is this all?"

"Yep. That's the lot of it."

I put the stapler back in the box. "So the whole thing would come to ¥6,800."

"Correct. ¥6,800. You're probably thinking, 'Well, okay, he shoplifted. It's a crime, sure, but why get so worked up about eight staplers? He's just a school kid.' Am I right?"

I didn't reply.

"It's okay to think that. 'Cause it's the truth. There are a lot worse crimes than stealing eight staplers. I was a policeman before I became a security guard, so I know what I'm talking about."

The guard looked directly into my eyes as he spoke. I held his gaze, careful not to appear defiant.

"If this were his first offence, the store wouldn't raise such a fuss. Our business is dealing with customers, after all, and we prefer not to get too upset over something small-scale like this. Normally I'd bring the child here to this room and I'd put a little of the fear of God into him. In worse cases we'd contact the parents and have them punish the child. We don't get in touch with the school. That's our store's policy, to take care of children shoplifting quietly.

"The problem is, this isn't the first time this boy's shoplifted. In our store alone we know he's done it three times. *Three times!* Can you imagine? And what's worse is both other times he refused to give us his name or the name of his school. I was the one who took care of him, so I remember it well. He wouldn't say a word, no matter what we asked. The silent treatment, we used to call it in the police force. No apologies, no remorse, just adopt a crummy attitude and stonewall it. If he didn't tell me his name this time, I was going to turn him over to the police, but even this didn't raise a reaction. Nothing else to do, so I forced him to show me his bus pass, and that's how I found out his name."

He paused, waiting for it all to sink in. He was still staring fixedly at me, and I continued to hold his gaze.

"Another thing is the kind of things he stole. Nothing cute about it. The first time he stole 15 propelling pencils. Total value, ¥9,750. The second time it was eight compasses, ¥8,000 altogether. In other words, each time he just steals a pile of the same things. He's not going to use them himself. He's just doing it for kicks, or else he's planning to sell it all to his friends at school."

I tried conjuring up a mental image of Carrot selling stolen staplers to his friends during lunch hour. I couldn't picture it.

"I don't quite understand," I said. "Why keep stealing from the same shop? Wouldn't that just increase the chances you'd get caught – and worsen your punishment when you were? If you're trying to get away with it, wouldn't you normally try other shops?"

"Don't ask me. Maybe he *was* stealing from other shops. Or maybe ours just happens to be his favourite. Maybe he doesn't like my face. I'm just a simple security guard for a supermarket, so I'm not going to think out all the ramifications. They don't pay me enough for that. If you really want to know, ask him yourself. I hauled him in here three hours ago and not a peep so far. Pretty amazing. Which is why I dragged you in here. I'm sorry you had to come in on your day off . . . One thing I've been wondering about since you came in, though. You look so tanned. Not that it's relevant, but did you go somewhere special for your summer holidays?"

"No, nowhere special," I replied.

Even so, he continued to scrutinize my face carefully, as if I were an important piece in the puzzle.

I picked up the stapler again and examined it in detail. Just an ordinary, small stapler, the kind you'd find in any home or office. An office supply about as cheap as they come.

Seven Star cigarette dangling from his lips, the security guard lit it with a Bic lighter and, turning to one side, blew out a cloud of smoke.

I turned to the boy and gently asked, "Why staplers?"

Carrot had been staring the whole time at the floor, but now he quietly lifted his face and looked at me. But he didn't say anything. I noticed for the first time that his expression was completely changed – strangely expressionless, eyes out of focus. He seemed to be staring into a void.

"Did somebody bully you into doing it?"

Still no answer. It was hard to tell if my words were getting through. I gave up. Asking the boy anything at this point wasn't going to be productive. His door was closed, the windows shut tight.

"Well, sir, what do you propose we do?" the guard asked me. "I get paid to make my rounds of the shop, check the monitors, catch shoplifters, and bring them back to this room. What happens afterwards is another matter entirely. Especially hard to deal with when it's a child. What do you suggest we do? I'm sure you're more knowledgeable in this area. Should we just let the police handle the whole thing? That would certainly be easier for me. Keep us from wasting our time when we're just treading water anyway."

Actually, at that moment I was thinking about something else. This dumpy little supermarket security room reminded me of the police station on the Greek island. Thoughts of which led straight to Sumire. And the fact that she was gone.

It took me a few moments to work out what this man was trying to say to me.

"I'll let his father know," Carrot's mother said in a monotone, "and make sure my son knows in no uncertain terms

204

that shoplifting is a crime. I promise he won't ever bother you again."

"In other words you don't want this to be taken to court. You've said that over and over," the security guard said in a bored tone. He tapped his cigarette on the ashtray, flicking the ash into it. He turned to me again and said, "But from where I sit, three times is just too many. Somebody's gotta put a stop to it. What are your feelings about this?"

I took a deep breath, pulling my thoughts back to the present. To the eight staplers and a Sunday afternoon in September.

"I can't say anything unless I talk to him," I replied. "He's a smart boy, and he's never caused any problems before. I have no clue why he'd do something so stupid, but I'm going to spend time myself and get to the bottom of this. I really apologize for all the trouble he's caused."

"Yeah, but I just don't get it," the guard said, frowning behind his glasses. "This boy – Shin'ichi Nimura? – he's in your class, right? So you see him every day, correct?"

"That's right."

"He's in fourth grade, which means he's been in your class for a year and four months. Am I right?"

"Yes, that's correct. I've been in charge of his class since they were in third grade."

"And how many pupils are in your class?"

"Thirty-five."

"So you can keep an eye on them all. You're telling me you never had any hint that this boy was going to cause trouble. No sign at all?"

"That's right."

"Wait a sec – as far as we know, he's been shoplifting for

205

a half year. Always alone. Nobody's threatening him to do it. And it's not spur of the moment. And he's not doing it for the money either. According to his mother he gets plenty of pocket money. He's doing it just to get away with stealing. This boy has *problems*, in other words. And you're telling me there wasn't any indication of this whatsoever?"

"I'm speaking as a teacher here," I replied, "but especially with children, habitual shoplifting is not so much a criminal act as the result of a subtle emotional imbalance. Maybe if I'd paid a little more attention I would have noticed something. I fell down on the job, definitely. But with emotionally disturbed children there's not always something outward to go on. If you separate the act from everything else and punish the child, the basic problem isn't going to be cured. Unless you find the fundamental cause and treat that, the same problem will surface later on in a different form. Often children are trying to send a message by shoplifting, so even if it isn't the most efficient way of handling the problem, it's important to take the time to talk things out."

The guard crushed out his cigarette and, mouth half open, stared at me for a long time, as if I were some odd-looking animal. His fingers resting on the tabletop were terribly thick, like ten little furry black creatures. The more I looked at them, the harder I found it to breathe.

"Is that what they teach you in college, in teacher-training or whatever you call it?"

"Not necessarily. It's basic psychology. You can find it in any book."

"You can find it in any book," he said, repeating my words listlessly. He picked up his hand towel and wiped away the sweat from his thick neck.

"A subtle emotional imbalance – what's *that* supposed to mean? When I was a policeman I spent every day, morning till night, dealing with characters who were imbalanced, all right. But there was nothing subtle about it. The world's full of people like that. Ten a penny. If I took the time to listen to each and every one of the messages those people were sending out, I'd need ten more brains. And that still wouldn't be enough."

He sighed, and placed the box of staplers back under the desk.

"Okay – you're absolutely right. Children have pure hearts. Corporal punishment is bad. People are all equal. You can't judge people by their grades. Take the time to talk and work out a solution. I don't have a major problem with that. But do you think that's how the world will get to be a better place? No way. It'll only get worse. How can people all be equal? I've never heard such a thing. Consider this – 110 million people are elbowing one another out of the way every day in Japan. Try making all of *them* equal. It'd be hell on earth.

"It's easy to say all these sweet words. Close your eyes, pretend not to see what's going on, and pass the buck. Don't make any waves, sing 'Auld Lang Syne', hand the kids their diplomas, and everybody lives happily ever after. Shoplifting is a child's message. Don't worry about later on. That's the easy way out, so why not? But who's going to clean up the mess? People like *me*, that's who. You think we do this because we like it? You lot have this kind of hey-what's-¥6,800?-look on your faces, but think about the people he stole from. A hundred people work here, and you better believe they take a difference of one or two yen

207

seriously. When they add up the receipts for a cash register and there's a ¥100 discrepancy, they work overtime to straighten it out. Do you know how much an hour the women who work the checkouts make here? Why don't you teach your pupils that?"

I didn't say anything. Carrot's mother was silent, as was the boy. The security guard had worn himself out talking and sank back into the general silence. In another room a phone rang, and someone picked it up on the first ring.

"So, what should we do?" he asked.

I said: "How about we string him upside down from the ceiling until he says he's sorry?"

"I like it! 'Course you know that we'd both be out on our ears."

"Well, then, the only thing we can do is patiently take the time to discuss the problem. That's all I can say."

Someone from another room knocked at the door and entered. "Mr Nakamura, could you lend me the key to the storeroom?" he asked. Mr Nakamura rummaged through the drawer in his desk for a while, but couldn't find it.

"It's gone," he said. "That's strange. I always keep it in here."

"It's very important," the other man said. "I need it now." The way the two of them talked about it, it sounded like a very important key, something that probably shouldn't have been kept in a drawer to begin with. They rifled through every drawer, but came up empty-handed.

The three of us just sat there while this was going on. A couple of times Carrot's mother glanced at me beseechingly. Carrot sat as before, expressionless, eyes pinned to the ground. Pointless, random thoughts flashed through my head. The room was stifling.

The man who needed the key gave up, grumbling as he left.

"That's enough," Mr Nakamura said, turning to us; in a toneless, matter-of-fact voice he continued: "Thank you for coming. We're finished here. I'll leave the rest up to you and the boy's mother. But get one thing clear – if he does this one more time, he won't get off this easy. You do understand that, I hope? I don't want any trouble. But I do have to do my job."

She nodded, and so did I. Carrot looked as though he hadn't heard a word. I stood up, and the two of them weakly followed suit.

"One last thing," the security guard said, still seated. He looked up at me. "I know this is rude of me, but I'll just go ahead and say it. Since I laid eyes on you there's something just not quite right. You're young, tall, make a good impression, nicely tanned, logical. Everything you say makes absolute sense. I'm sure the parents of your pupils like you a lot. I can't really explain it, but since I first saw you something's been gnawing at me. Something I just can't swallow. Nothing personal, so don't get angry. It's just something bothers me. But what is it that's gnawing at me, I wonder?"

"Would you mind if I ask you something personal?" I said.

"Ask away."

"If people aren't equal, where would you fit in?"

Mr Nakamura took a deep lungful of cigarette smoke, shook his head, and exhaled ever so slowly, as if he were forcing someone to do something. "I don't know," he replied.

"Don't you worry, though. The two of us won't be sharing the same level."

She'd parked her red Toyota Celica in the supermarket car park. I called her over to one side, away from her son, and told her to go on home alone.

"I need to talk to your son alone for a while," I said. "I'll bring him home later." She nodded. She was about to say something, but didn't, got in her car, took her sunglasses from her bag, and started the engine.

After she left I took Carrot to a cheerful-looking little coffee shop I noticed nearby. I relaxed in the air-conditioning, ordered an iced tea for myself and an ice-cream for the boy. I undid the top button of my shirt, took off my tie, and slipped it in my jacket pocket. Carrot remained sunk in silence. His expression and the look in his eyes were unchanged from when we were in the security office. He looked completely blank, like he was going to be that way for a while. His small hands placed neatly in his lap, he looked down at the floor, averting his face. I drank my iced tea, but Carrot didn't touch his ice-cream. It slowly melted in the dish, but he didn't seem to notice. We sat facing each other like some married couple sharing an awkward silence. Every time she stopped by our table, the waitress looked tense.

"Things just happen," I said finally. I wasn't trying to break the ice. The words just came bubbling up.

Carrot slowly raised his head and turned towards me. He didn't say a thing. I shut my eyes, sighed, and was silent for a while.

"I haven't told anybody yet," I said, "but during the

summer holidays I went to Greece. You know where Greece is, don't you? We watched that video in social studies class, remember? In southern Europe, next to the Mediterranean. They have lots of islands and grow olives. Five hundred BC was the peak of their civilization. Athens was the birthplace of democracy, and Socrates took poison and died. That's where I went. It's a beautiful place. But I didn't go to have a good time. A friend of mine disappeared on a small Greek island, and I went to help search. But we didn't find anything. My friend just quietly vanished. Like smoke."

Carrot opened his mouth a crack and looked at me. His expression was still hard and lifeless, but a glimmer of light appeared. I'd got through to him.

"I really liked this friend of mine. Very, very much. My friend was the most important person in the world to me. So I took a plane to Greece to help search. But it didn't help. We didn't find a clue. Since I lost my friend, I don't have any more friends. Not a single one."

I wasn't talking to Carrot as much as to myself. Thinking aloud.

"You know what I'd really like to do the most right now? Climb up to the top of some high place like the pyramids. The highest place I can find. Where you can see as far as possible. Stand on the very top, look all around the world, see all the scenery, and see with my own eyes what's been lost from the world. I don't know . . . Maybe I really don't want to see that. Maybe I don't want to see anything any more."

The waitress came over, removed Carrot's plate of melted ice cream, and left the bill.

"I feel like I've been alone ever since I was a child. I had parents and an older sister at home, but I didn't get along with them. I couldn't communicate with anyone in my family. So I often imagined I was adopted. For some reason some distant relatives gave me up to my family. Or maybe they got me from an orphanage. Now I realize how silly that idea was. My parents aren't the type to adopt a helpless orphan. Anyway, I couldn't accept the fact that I was related by blood to these people. It was easier to think they were complete strangers.

"I imagined a town far away. There was a house there, where my real family lived. Just a modest little house, but warm and inviting. Everyone there can understand one another, they say whatever they feel like. In the evening you can hear Mum bustling around in the kitchen getting dinner ready, and there's a warm, delicious fragrance. *That's* where I belong. I was always picturing this place in my mind, with me as a part of the picture.

"In real life my family had a dog, and he was the only one I got along with. He was a mongrel, but pretty bright; once you taught him something he never forgot. I took him for a walk every day, and we'd go to the park; I'd sit on a bench and talk about all sorts of things. We understood each other. Those were my happiest moments as a child. When I was in fifth grade my dog was hit by a lorry near our house and killed. My parents wouldn't let me buy another. They're too noisy and dirty, they told me, too much trouble.

"After my dog died I stayed in my room a lot, just reading books. The world in books seemed so much more alive to me than anything outside. I could see things I'd never seen before. Books and music were my best friends. I had a couple of good friends at school, but never met anyone I could really speak my heart to. We'd just make small talk, play football together. When something bothered me, I didn't talk with anyone about it. I thought it over all by myself, came to a conclusion, and took action alone. Not that I really felt lonely. I thought that's just the way things are. Human beings, in the final analysis, have to survive on their own.

"When I entered college, though, I made a friend, the one I told you about. And my way of thinking started to change. I came to understand that thinking just by myself for so long was holding me back, keeping me to a single viewpoint. And I started to feel that being all alone is a terribly lonely thing.

"Being all alone is like the feeling you get when you stand at the mouth of a large river on a rainy evening and watch the water flow into the sea. Have you ever done that? Stand at the mouth of a large river and watch the water flow into the sea?"

Carrot didn't reply.

"*I* have," I said.

Eyes wide open, Carrot looked in my face.

"I can't really say why it's such a lonely feeling to watch all the river water mix together with the sea water. But it really is. You should try it sometime."

I picked up my jacket and the bill and slowly stood up. I rested a hand on Carrot's shoulder, and he got up, too. And we left the coffee shop.

It took about 30 minutes to walk to his house. We walked together, and I didn't say a word.

Near his house was a small river, with a concrete bridge over it. A bland little thing, really, less a river than a drainage ditch that had been widened. When there was still farmland around here it must have been used for irrigation. Now, though, the water was cloudy, with a slight odour of detergent. Summer grasses sprouted in the riverbed, a discarded comic book lay open in the water. Carrot came to a halt in the middle of the bridge, leaned over the railing, and gazed down. I stood beside him and looked down, too. We stood like that for a long time. He probably didn't want to go back home. I could understand that.

Carrot stuck a hand inside his trouser pocket, pulled out a key, and held it towards me. Just an ordinary key, with a large red tag on it. The tag said STORAGE 3 on it. The key for the storeroom that the security guard, Nakamura, was looking for. Carrot must have been left alone in the room for a moment, found it in the drawer, and slipped it into his pocket. This boy's mind was a bigger enigma than I'd imagined. He was an altogether strange child.

I took the key and held it in my palm and could feel the weight of countless people that had seeped into it. It struck me as terribly wretched, dirty, small-minded. Flustered for a moment, I ended up dropping the key into the river. It made a tiny splash. The river wasn't very deep, but the water was cloudy, and the key disappeared from sight. Side by side on the bridge, Carrot and I gazed at the water for a time. Somehow it made me feel cheerful, my body lighter.

"It's too late to take it back," I said, more to myself than to him. "I'm sure they have a spare somewhere. It's their precious *storeroom*, after all."

I held my hand out, and Carrot softly took it in his. I could feel his slim, small fingers in mine. A feeling that I'd experienced somewhere – where could it have been? – a long long time ago. I held his hand and we headed for his home.

His mother was waiting for us when we got there. She'd changed into a smart little white, sleeveless blouse and a pleated skirt. Her eyes were red and swollen. She must have cried alone the whole time after she got home. Her husband ran an estate agent's in the city and on Sundays was either at work or out playing golf. She had Carrot go to his room on the first floor and took me not to the living room, but to the kitchen, where we sat down at the table. Maybe it was easier for her to talk there. The kitchen had a huge avocado-green fridge, an island in the middle, and a sunny window facing east.

"He looks a little better than he did before," she said weakly. "When I first saw him at that security office, I didn't know what to do. I've never seen him look that way. Like he was off in another world."

"There's nothing to worry about. Just give it time and he'll get back to normal. For the time being it'd be better if you don't say anything to him. Just leave him alone."

"What did you two do after I left?"

"We talked," I said.

"About what?"

"Not much. Basically I did all the talking. Nothing special, really."

"Would you like something cold to drink?"

I shook my head.

"I have no idea how to talk to him any more," she said. "And that feeling just grows stronger."

"There's no need to force yourself to talk to him. Children are in their own world. When he wants to talk, he will."

"But he barely talks at all."

We were careful not to let our bodies touch as we faced each other across the kitchen table. Our conversation was strained, the kind you might expect of a teacher and a mother discussing a problem child. As she spoke she played with her hands, twisting her fingers, stretching them out, grasping her hands. I thought about the things those hands had done to me in bed.

I won't report what's happened to the school, I told her. I'll have a good talk with him, and if there's any problem, I'll take care of it. So don't worry about it. He's a smart boy, a good boy; give it time and he'll settle down. This is just a phase he's going through. The most important thing is for you to be calm about it. I slowly, calmly repeated all this over and over, letting it sink in. It seemed to make her feel better.

She said she'd drive me back to my apartment in Kunitachi.

"Do you think my son senses what's going on?" she asked me when we were stopped at a traffic light. What she meant, of course, was what was going on between her and me.

I shook my head. "Why do you say that?"

"While I was alone at home, waiting for you to come back, the thought just struck me. I have nothing to go by, it's just a feeling. He's very intuitive, and I'm sure he's picked up on how my husband and I don't get along well."

I was silent. She didn't say any more.

She parked her car in the car park just beyond the intersection where my apartment building stood. She pulled on the handbrake and turned off the engine. It sputtered out, and with the sound from the air-conditioning off, an uncomfortable silence fell over the car. I knew she wanted me to take her in my arms right then and there. I thought of her pliant body beneath her blouse, and my mouth became dry.

"I think it'd be better for us not to meet any more," I came right out and said.

She didn't say anything. Hands on the steering wheel, she stared in the direction of the oil gauge. Almost all expression had faded from her face.

"I've given it a lot of thought," I said. "I don't think it's right that I'm part of the problem. I can't be part of the solution if I'm part of the problem. It's better for everyone that way."

"Everyone?"

"Especially for your son."

"For you, too?"

"Yes. Of course."

"What about me? Does that include me?"

Yes, I wanted to say. But I couldn't get the word out. She took off her dark green Raybans, then slipped them on again.

"It's not easy for me to say this," she said, "but if I can't see you any more it will be very hard on me."

"It will be hard on me, too. I wish we could continue the way we are. But it's not right."

She took a deep breath and let it out.

"What is right? Would you tell me? I don't really know

217

what's right. I know what's wrong. But what is *right*?"

I didn't have a good answer.

She looked like she was about to weep. Or cry out. But somehow she held herself in check. She just gripped the steering wheel tightly, the backs of her hands turning slightly red.

"When I was younger all kinds of people talked to me," she said. "Told me all sorts of things. Fascinating stories, beautiful, strange stories. But past a certain point nobody talked to me any more. No one. Not my husband, my child, my friends . . . no one. Like there was nothing left in the world to talk about. Sometimes I feel like my body's turning invisible, like you can see right through me."

She raised her hands from the steering wheel and held them out in front of her.

"Not that you would understand what I'm trying to say."

I searched for the right words, but nothing came.

"Thank you very much for everything today," she said, pulling herself together. Her voice was nearly her usual, calm tone. "I don't think I could have handled it alone. It's very hard on me. Having you there helped a lot. I'm grateful. I know you're going to be a wonderful teacher. You almost are."

Was this meant to be sarcastic? Probably. No – definitely.

"Not yet," I said. She smiled, ever so slightly. And our conversation came to an end.

I opened the car door and stepped outside. The summer Sunday afternoon sunlight had weakened considerably. I found it hard to breathe and my legs felt strange as I stood there. The Celica's engine roared to life, and she drove out of my life for ever. She rolled down her window and gave a small wave, and I lifted my hand in response.

Back in the apartment I took off my sweaty shirt and tossed it in the washing machine, took a shower, and washed my hair. I went to the kitchen, finished preparing the meal I'd left half done, and ate. Afterwards, I sank back in my sofa and read a book I'd just started. But I couldn't finish five pages. Giving up, I closed the book and thought for a while about Sumire. And the storeroom key I'd tossed in the filthy river. And my girlfriend's hands gripping the steering wheel. It had been a long day, and it was finally over, leaving behind just random memories. I'd taken a good long shower, but my body was still steeped in the stink of tobacco. And my hand still retained a sharp sensation – as if I'd crushed the life out of something.

Did I do what was *right?*

I didn't think so. I'd only done what was necessary for *me*. There's a big difference. *Everyone?* she'd asked me. *Does that include me?*

Truthfully, at that time I wasn't thinking about everyone. I was thinking only about Sumire. Not all of *them* there, or all of *us* here.

Only of Sumire, who wasn't anywhere.

16

I hadn't heard a word from Miu since the day we'd said goodbye at the harbour. This struck me as odd, since she promised to get in touch regardless of whether there was any news about Sumire. I couldn't believe she'd forgotten me; she wasn't the type to make promises she didn't intend to keep. Something must have happened to keep her from contacting me. I considered calling her, but I didn't even know her real name, or the name of her company or where it was. As far as Miu was concerned, Sumire hadn't left behind any solid leads.

Sumire's phone still had the same message on it, but it was soon disconnected. I thought about calling her family. I didn't know the number, though it wouldn't have been hard to find her father's dental clinic in the Yokohama Yellow Pages. But somehow I couldn't take that step. Instead, I went to the library and looked through the August newspapers. There was a tiny article about her, about a 22-year-old

Japanese girl travelling in Greece who disappeared. The local authorities are investigating, searching for her. But so far no clues. That was it. Nothing I didn't already know. Quite a few people travelling abroad disappeared, it seemed. And she was merely one of them.

I gave up trying to follow the news. Whatever the reasons for her disappearance, however the investigation was proceeding, one thing was certain: if Sumire were to come back, she'd get in touch. That was all that mattered.

September came and went, autumn was over before I knew it, and winter set in. 7 November was Sumire's 23rd birthday, and 9 December was my 25th. The New Year came and the school year ended. Carrot didn't cause any more problems and went into fifth grade, into a new class. After that day I never really talked to him about the shoplifting. Every time I saw him, I realized it wasn't necessary.

Since he had a new teacher now, there were fewer times I'd come across my former girlfriend. Everything was over and done with. Sometimes, though, a nostalgic memory of the warmth of her skin would come to me, and I'd be on the verge of picking up the phone. What brought me to a halt was the feeling of that supermarket storeroom key in my hand. Of that summer afternoon. And of Carrot's little hand in mine.

Every time I met Carrot at school, I couldn't help thinking that he was one strange child. I had no inkling of what thoughts were brewing behind that thin, calm face. But something was definitely going on under that placid exterior. And if push came to shove, he had the wherewithal to take action. I could sense something deep about him. I believed that telling him the feelings I held inside was the right thing to do. For him, and for me. Probably more for my sake. It's a little strange to say this, but he understood me then and accepted me. And even forgave me. To some extent, at least.

What kind of days – the seemingly endless days of youth – would children like Carrot go through as they grew into adulthood? It wouldn't be easy for them. Hard times would outnumber the easy. From my own experience, I could predict the shape their pain would take. Would he fall in love with somebody? And would that other person love him back? Not that my thinking about it mattered. Once he graduated from elementary school, he'd be gone, and I'd see him no more. And I had my own problems to think about.

I went to a record shop, bought a copy of Elisabeth Schwarzkopf singing Mozart's lieder, and listened to it again and again. I loved the beautiful stillness of the songs. If I closed my eyes, the music always took me back to that night on the Greek island.

Aside from some very vivid memories, including the one of the overwhelming desire I felt the day I helped her move, all Sumire left behind were several long letters and the floppy disk. I read the letters and the two documents so many times I nearly had them memorized. Every time I read them, I felt like Sumire and I were together again, our hearts one. This warmed my heart more than anything else could. Like you're on a train at night travelling across some vast plain, and you catch a glimpse of a tiny light in the window of a farmhouse. In an instant it's sucked back into the darkness behind and vanishes. But if you close your eyes, that point of light stays with you, just barely, for a few moments.

I wake up in the middle of the night and get out of bed (I'm not going to be able to sleep anyway), lie down on my sofa, and relive memories of that small Greek island as I listen to Schwarzkopf. I recollect each and every event, quietly turning the pages of my memory. The lovely deserted beach, the outdoor café at the harbour. The waiter's sweat-stained shirt. Miu's graceful profile and the sparkle of the Mediterranean from the veranda. The poor hero standing in the town square who'd been impaled. And the Greek music I heard from the mountaintop that night. I vividly relive the magical moonlight, the wondrous echo of the music. The sensation of estrangement I experienced when I was awakened by the music. That formless, midnight pain, like my body, too, was silently, cruelly, being impaled

Lying there, I close my eyes for a while, then open them. I silently breathe in, then out. A thought begins to form in my mind, but in the end I think of nothing. Not that there was much difference between the two, thinking and not thinking. I find I can no longer distinguish between one thing and another, between things that existed and things that did not. I look out the window. Until the sky turns white, clouds float by, birds chirp, and a new day lumbers up, gathering together the sleepy minds of the people who inhabit this planet.

Once in downtown Tokyo I caught a glimpse of Miu. It was about six months after Sumire disappeared, a warm Sunday in the middle of March. Low clouds covered the sky, and it looked like it would rain at any minute. Everyone carried umbrellas. I was on my way to visit some relatives who lived downtown and was stopped at a traffic light in Hiroo, at the intersection near the MEIDI-YA store, when I spotted the navy-blue Jaguar inching its way forward in the heavy traffic. I was in a taxi, and the Jaguar was in the through lane to my left. I noticed the car because its driver was a woman with a stunning mane of white hair. From a distance, her white hair stood out starkly against the flawless navy-blue car. I had only seen Miu with black hair, so it took me a while to put this Miu and the Miu I knew together. But it was definitely her. She was as beautiful as I remembered, refined in a rare and wonderful way. Her breathtaking white hair kept one at arm's length and had a resolute, almost mythical air about it.

The Miu before me, though, was not the woman I had waved goodbye to at the harbour on the Greek island. Only half a year had passed, yet she looked like a different person. Of course her hair colour was changed. But that wasn't all.

An empty shell. Those were the first words that sprang to mind. Miu was like an empty room after everyone's left. Something incredibly important – the same something that pulled in Sumire like a tornado, that shook my heart as I stood on the deck of the ferry – had disappeared from Miu for good. Leaving behind not life, but its absence. Not the warmth of something alive, but the silence of memory. Her pure-white hair inevitably made me imagine the colour of human bones, bleached by the passage of time. For a time, I couldn't exhale.

The Jaguar Miu was driving sometimes got ahead of my taxi, sometimes fell behind, but Miu didn't notice I was watching her from nearby. I couldn't call out to her. I didn't know what to say, but even if I had, the windows of the Jaguar were shut tight. Miu was sitting up straight, both hands on the steering wheel, her attention fixed on the scene ahead of her. She might have been thinking deeply about something. Or maybe she was listening to the "Art of the Fugue" that was playing on her car stereo. The entire time her icy, hardened expression didn't change, and she barely blinked. Finally the light turned green and the Jaguar sped off in the direction of Aoyama, leaving behind my taxi, which sat there waiting to make a right turn.

So that's how we live our lives. No matter how deep and fatal the loss, no matter how important the thing that's stolen from us – that's snatched right out of our hands – even if we are left completely changed people with only the outer layer of skin from before, we continue to play out our lives this way, in silence. We draw ever nearer to our allotted span of time, bidding it farewell as it trails off behind. Repeating, often adroitly, the endless deeds of the everyday. Leaving behind a feeling of immeasurable emptiness.

Though she came back to Japan, Miu couldn't get in touch with me for some reason. Instead, she kept her silence, clutching her memories close, seeking some nameless, remote place to swallow her up. That's what I imagined. I didn't feel like blaming Miu. Let alone hating her.

The image that came to mind at that moment was of the bronze statue of Miu's father in the little mountain village in North Korea. I could picture the tiny town square, the low-slung houses, and the dust-covered bronze statue. The

225

wind always blows hard there, twisting the trees into surreal shapes. I don't know why, but that bronze statue and Miu, hands on the steering wheel of her Jaguar, melted into one in my mind.

Maybe, in some distant place, everything is already, quietly, lost. Or at least there exists a silent place where everything can disappear, melding together in a single, overlapping figure. And as we live our lives we discover – drawing towards us the thin threads attached to each – what has been lost. I closed my eyes and tried to bring to mind as many beautiful lost things as I could. Drawing them closer, holding on to them. Knowing all the while that their lives are fleeting.

I dream. Sometimes I think that's the only right thing to do. To dream, to live in the world of dreams – just as Sumire said. But it doesn't last for ever. Wakefulness always comes to take me back.

I wake up at 3 a.m., turn on the light, sit up, and look at the phone beside my bed. I picture Sumire in a phone box, lighting up a cigarette and pushing the buttons for my number. Her hair's a mess; she has on a man's herringbone jacket many sizes too big for her and mismatched socks. She frowns, choking a bit on the smoke. It takes her a long time to push all the numbers correctly. Her head is crammed full of things she wants to tell me. She might talk until dawn, who knows? About the difference, say, between symbols and signs. My phone looks as though it will ring any minute now. But it doesn't ring. I lie down and stare at the silent phone.

But one time it does ring. Right in front of me, it actually

226

rings. Making the air of the real world tremble and shake. I grab the receiver.

"Hello?"

"Hey, I'm back," said Sumire. Very casual. Very real. "It wasn't easy, but somehow I managed it. Like a 50-word précis of Homer's *Odyssey*."

"That's good," I said. I still couldn't believe it. Being able to hear her voice. The fact that this was happening.

"That's good?" Sumire said, and I could almost hear the frown. "What the heck do you mean by that? I've gone through bloody hell, I'll have you know. The obstacles I went through – millions of them, I'd never finish if I tried to explain them all – all this to get back, and that's all you can say? I think I'm going to cry. If it isn't *good* that I'm back, where would that leave me? *That's good*. I can't believe it! Save that kind of heartwarming, witty remark for the kids in your class – when they finally work out how to multiply!"

"Where are you now?"

"Where am I? Where do you think I am? In our good old faithful telephone box. This crummy little square telephone box plastered inside with ads for phony loan companies and escort services. A mouldy-coloured half-moon's hanging in the sky; the floor's littered with cigarette butts. As far as the eye can see, nothing to warm the cockles of the heart. An interchangeable, totally semiotic telephone box. So, where is it? I'm not exactly sure. Everything's just too semiotic – and you know me, right? I don't know where I am half the time. I can't give directions well. Taxi drivers are always yelling at me: *Hey lady, where in the world you trying to get to?* I'm not too far away, I think. Probably pretty close by."

"I'll come and get you."

"I'd like that. I'll find out where I am and call you back. I'm running out of change, anyway. Wait for a while, okay?"

"I really wanted to see you," I said.

"And I really wanted to see you, too," she said. "When I couldn't see you any more, I realized that. It was as clear as if the planets all of a sudden lined up in a row for me. I really need you. You're a part of me; I'm a part of you. You know, somewhere – I'm not at all sure where – I think I cut something's throat. Sharpening my knife, my heart a stone. Symbolically, like making a gate in China. Do you understand what I'm saying?"

"I think so."

"Then come and get me."

Suddenly the phone cuts off. Still clutching the receiver, I stare at it for a long time. Like the phone itself is some vital message, its very shape and colour containing hidden meaning. Reconsidering, I hang up. I sit up in bed and wait for the phone to ring again. I lean back against the wall, my focus fixed on a single point in the space before me, and I breathe slowly, soundlessly. Making sure of the joints bridging one moment of time and the next. The phone doesn't ring. An unconditional silence hangs in the air. But I'm in no hurry. There's no need to rush. I'm ready. I can go anywhere.

Right?
Right you are!

I get up out of bed. I pull back the old, faded curtain and open the window. I stick my head out and look up at the sky. Sure enough, a mouldy-coloured half-moon hangs in the sky. *Good*. We're both looking at the same moon, in the same world. We're connected to reality by the same line. All I have to do is quietly draw it towards me.

I spread my fingers apart and stare at the palms of both hands, looking for bloodstains. There aren't any. No scent of blood, no stiffness. The blood must have already, in its own silent way, seeped inside.

Also available by Haruki Murakami

THE WIND-UP BIRD CHRONICLE

'Mesmerising, surreal, this really is the work of a true
original'
The Times

'Murakami writes of contemporary Japan, urban alienation
and journey's of self-discovery, and in this book he com-
bines recollections of the war with metaphysics, dreams and
hallucinations into a powerful and impressionistic work'
Independent

Toru Okada's cat has disappeared and this has unsettled his
wife, who is herself growing more distant every day. Then
there are the increasingly explicit telephone calls he has
started receiving. As this compelling story unfolds, the tidy
suburban realities of Okada's vague and blameless life,
spent cooking, reading, listening to jazz and opera and
drinking beer at the kitchen table, are turned inside out, and
he embarks on a bizarre journey, guided (however
obscurely) by a succession of characters, each with a tale to
tell.

'Murakami weaves these textured layers of reality into a
shot-silk garment of deceptive beauty'
Independent on Sunday

VINTAGE

Also available by Haruki Murakami

NORWEGIAN WOOD

'Murakami must already rank among the world's greatest living novelists'
Guardian

'Evocative, entertaining, sexy and funny; but then Murakami is one of the best writers around'
Time Out

'Such is the exquisite, gossamer construction of Murakami's writing that everything he chooses to describe trembles with symbolic possibility'
Guardian

When he hears her favourite Beatles song, Toru Watanabe recalls his first love Naoko, the girlfriend of his best friend Kizuki. Immediately he is transported back almost twenty years to his student days in Tokyo, adrift in a world of uneasy friendships, casual sex, passion, loss and desire – to a time when an impetuous young woman called Midori marches into his life and he has to choose between the future and the past.

'This book is undeniably hip, full of student uprisings, free love, booze and 1960s pop, it's also genuinely emotionally engaging, and describes the highs of adolescence as well as the lows'
Independent on Sunday

VINTAGE

BY HARUKI MURAKAMI
ALSO AVAILABLE FROM VINTAGE

☐	after the Quake	0099448564	£6.99
☐	Dance Dance Dance	0099448769	£7.99
☐	The Elephant Vanishes	0099448750	£7.99
☐	Hard-boiled Wonderland and the End of the World	0099448785	£7.99
☐	Norwegian Wood	0099448823	£7.99
☐	South of the Border, West of the Sun	0099448572	£6.99
☐	Underground	0099461099	£7.99
☐	A Wild Sheep Chase	0099448777	£7.99
☐	The Wind-up Bird Chronicle	0099448793	£7.99
☐	Kafka on the Shore	0099458322	£7.99
☐	Birthday Stories	0099481553	£7.99